THIS BOOK BELONGS TO:

Draw yourself (or write your name) here if you own this book.

The Accidental Diary of B.U.G.

Jen Carney

PUFFIN

PUFFIN BOOKS

UK | USA | Canada | Ireland | Australia
India | New Zealand | South Africa

Puffin Books is part of the Penguin Random House group of companies
whose addresses can be found at global.penguinrandomhouse.com.

www.penguin.co.uk
www.puffin.co.uk
www.ladybird.co.uk

First published 2021

003

Text design by Janene Spencer
Printed in Great Britain by Clays Ltd, Elcograf S.p.A.

The authorized representative in the EEA is Penguin Random House Ireland,
Morrison Chambers, 32 Nassau Street, Dublin D02 YH68

A CIP catalogue record for this book is available from the British Library

ISBN: 978-0-241-45544-9

All correspondence to:
Puffin Books
Penguin Random House Children's
One Embassy Gardens, 8 Viaduct Gardens, London SW11 7BW

For Michael and Vickie —
the first pair of #BFFs I ever knew

NEVER 'BUG' ME

Hello! My name is **B**elinda **U**pton **G**reen and my number-one rule, which I'll make perfectly clear before we go any further, is:

DON'T EVER CALL ME **BUG**!

Well, how would you like it if someone called you by your initials? Most of you would be called ridiculous, impossible-to-pronounce things like Hjm or Evbc or Vms. But what about your friends with names such as **P**enelope **O**livia **O**rwell or **B**obby **U**nderwood-**M**iller? They'd be even more embarrassed than me.

You get my point . . .

PENELOPE

In my opinion, you should only allow this very silly NICKNAME TREND, which went round my SCHOOL last week, if you're lucky enough to be called something like **A**nthony **C**harles **E**gan or **E**liza **P**oppy **I**sobelle **C**arter.

FREDERICK

Don't say I didn't warn you.
Especially you, **F**rederick
Archibald **R**ushton-**T**arbuck!

Anyway, you can call me Billie.

DECISIONS, DECISIONS

I totally know how annoying it can be to begin a new book and only realize at Page 10 that it's not actually your cup of tea, so, now that I've politely introduced myself, I'm about to do you a HUGE favour before we get down to the nitty-gritty.

Here are four decision charts (all unscientifically proven) to help people who find EXTREMELY important decisions a bit tricky. Like me . . .

Don't worry – the questions are EASY–PEASY and basically your answers will 100% help you decide whether to give up or dive further in.

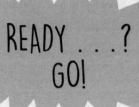

READY . . .?
GO!

SHOULD YOU READ THIS BOOK DECISION MAKER (1)

WHAT KIND OF BOOKS
DO YOU USUALLY ENJOY?

Funny ones that make me laugh out loud and have interesting doodles and pictures in them.

VERY SERIOUS ONES WITH TONS OF LONG WORDS.

I don't like books.

Read the book immediately and demand a refund if you don't laugh 59 times.

Err . . . read the book to see if you know the longest word I know (it has 45 letters – seriously).

Hmm . . . read the book, then come back to this page and see if your answer has changed.

SHOULD YOU READ THIS BOOK DECISION MAKER (2)

SHOULD YOU READ THIS BOOK DECISION MAKER (3)

ARE YOU COOL?

YES → Read the book ... Cool people love it.

NO → Read the book to get cooler.

SHOULD YOU READ THIS BOOK DECISION MAKER (4)

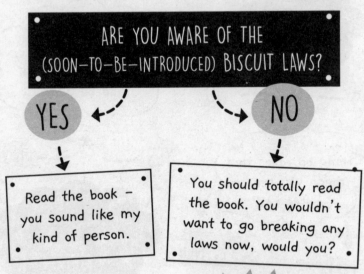

ARE YOU AWARE OF THE (SOON-TO-BE-INTRODUCED) BISCUIT LAWS?

YES → Read the book - you sound like my kind of person.

NO → You should totally read the book. You wouldn't want to go breaking any laws now, would you?

Made your decision?
Ready to start for real?

LET'S GO!

NEW INVENTION

MRS GREEN! CAN I HAVE A QUIET WORD?

I'll let you in on a secret . . . Mum bought me this jotter last week after my teacher felt the need to call her in for a quiet word. Which, by the way, was:

I. NOT AT ALL QUIET, and
2. DEFINITELY MORE THAN ONE WORD.

She told me it was for practising my SPELLINGS . . .

As that sounded like the WORST IDEA EVER, I've decided to put it to much better use. I mean, how could it be AT ALL time-wasty to invent an alien-cow-puppy instead of practising a frankly ridiculous set of words?

LOOK →

Right now it's Sunday night and, as usual,
Mum has sent me up to bed at what she calls
'A REASONABLE HOUR', but what is actually
'TOO EARLY TO EVEN THINK ABOUT PYJAMAS'.
I expect she thinks I'm fast asleep already,
but look – I'm under my covers, writing in
this jotter (which will *probably* contain one
of the SPELLINGS I need to learn at some point)
so it's basically her fault I'm wide awake IMHO.

Snug as a b**
in a rug!

In fact . . .

TOTALLY EXCELLENT
IDEA ALERT!

GOODBYE, dreadfully depressing SPELLINGS jotter.
HELLO, incredibly handy STAY-AWAKE DOODLE
DIARY.

RESULT!

Spellings Jotter

S.A.D. DIARY

FORBIDDEN SNACK

A totally AMAZING thing happened at morning break today. Layla had two actual genuine real-life Jaffa Cakes for her snack!

LAYLA

JAFFA CAKES OMG

I couldn't believe my eyes when she showed me.

YOU'RE LYING.

'Hide them quick!' I whispered, checking to see if a teacher was nearby.

Now I know this might sound a bit extreme but since my school introduced this completely INSANE rule we've had to be on our guard.

SCHOOL RULES (456–458)

456 NO HOPPING IN P.E.

457 TRANSPARENT LUNCH BOXES ONLY

458 MORNING-BREAK SNACK MUST ALWAYS BE HEALTHY!

Last week Dale Redman had a cereal bar with the teeniest-tiniest bit of chocolate on it confiscated, so, although they **definitely** contain oranges, I knew for sure and certain the Jaffa Cakes would be considered HIGHLY ILLEGAL.

Layla immediately stuffed them up her jumper and pulled me over to the big tree near the railings so we could figure out what to do.

CONFIDENTIAL DISCUSSIONS

You should probably know that, as well as being 100% #BFFs, Layla Dixon and I ALWAYS share snacks. We find it keeps morning break interesting. Well, as interesting as it can be now chocolate and crisps have been banned. I get the better deal most days if I'm honest, as Layla's mum often packs her snacks like yoghurt-covered raisins (basically sweets) and Cheestrings (basically toys), whereas I'm usually lumbered with things like plain rice cakes (aka cardboard) or slices of apple (brown by break time).

We made a PROMISE, though, and we both keep to it.

Unfortunately, Patrick North was already behind the big tree looking for worms. Patrick North is the biggest PEST in Class Five.

PATRICK NORTH

'Hello, Lid and Bug!' he said. 'What are you two doing?'

Patrick tells tales about absolutely everything (once, and this is 100% true, he complained to Mrs Patterson that I'd **'looked at him'**) so we knew we couldn't enjoy our illegal snack there.

CRIME OF THE CENTURY

'DO NOT call me Bug!' I shouted, before grabbing Layla's hand and running towards the girls' cloakroom.

Layla's middle name is Imogen and, although Lid is nowhere

near as bad as Bug, she's also banned people from calling

LAYLA

her by her initials because that's what #BFFs do. We stick together.

ME

When we got to the cloakroom, Daisy Muirhead and Farida Banerjee were there practising their seven times tables in preparation for the test Mrs Patterson had announced would happen after break. Seriously, WHO CARES who can work out seven times eight the fastest?

7×8?

52?

That's what calculators were invented for.

(As well as making words out of numbers - obviously.)

BOOBLESS

8008

'Hi, Bug!' said Farida. (Farida Banerjee is desperate for the initials-as-your-nickname thing to stick. She says her middle name is Anita . . . I bet it's actually Ingrid.)

'Stop calling her that!' said Layla, distracting me from getting into an argument with Farida by showing me the time on her watch.

It was getting seriously near the end of break — this was becoming an

EMERGENCY SITUATION!

I expect you're wondering why we didn't simply stuff the Jaffa Cakes into our mouths and hope for the best. Well, I'll tell you. That, my friend, would have involved us breaking one of the extremely serious BISCUIT LAWS we developed during a completely crumby (but mega marvellous) sleepover last year:

BISCUIT LAWS

1. **THE CREAM-FILLED COMMANDMENT** (for things like custard creams): Thou shalt ALWAYS remove the top layer and scrape out the cream with thy teeth.

2. **THE LICK-IT-ALL-OFF LAW** (for things like chocolate digestives): Every last scrap of chocolate must be removed with the tongue before eating (or binning) the BISCUIT.

3. **THE COMPLETELY-DECONSTRUCT-IT CHARTER** (mainly for Jaffa Cakes): Thou shalt endeavour to take it apart completely, saving the sweet disc of jelly till last.

4. **THE CODE OF REMOVAL** (this applies to things like Clubs): Without fail, thou shalt nibble off as much chocolate as possible before eating the remaining BISCUIT.

5. **THE DUNKING DEMAND** (for anything dullish like a rich tea): Thou must always dunk it - preferably in a large mug of hot chocolate.

We're still waiting to hear back from the prime minister about these laws but to ensure you're ready for when they become compulsory I suggest you immediately ask an adult for one of each variety so you can practise.

Anyway . . .

Back to break time . . .

Our last option was the girls' toilets.

It was mega ~~unhijeanik~~ ~~unhyjeenic~~ grubby to deconstruct our illegal discs of chocolatey-orangey-cakey-BISCUITY heaven in a toilet cubicle, but it was totally worth it.

Jaffa Cakes are ULTRA AMAZING and swapping three wrinkly carrot batons for one disc of heaven was an EPICALLY EXCELLENT EXCHANGE.

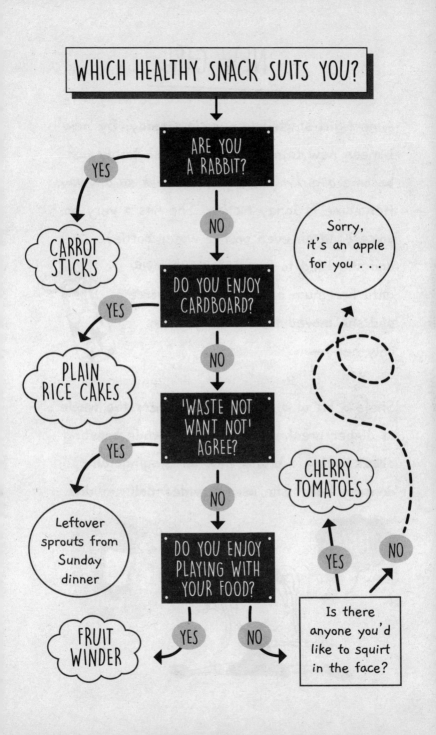

NEW GIRL

A new girl started in our class today. By 'new'
I mean new to our class; she hasn't only just
become a girl – well, I don't think so anyway.
Her name is Janey McVey. She has a very posh
voice (and an even posher water bottle)
and she used to live 356 miles away
until her mum and dad got a divorce
and she moved to our village with
only her mum.

She's a bit of a show-off and spent the whole
of dinner break doing the splits while boasting
about having a brand-new all-singing, all-
dancing tablet she uses to video-call her dad.

JANEY

Everyone in Class Five thought Janey McVey was pretty and I suppose she is in her own brand-new-uniform-and-two-scrunchies way. Judging people on their appearance is something I try not to do . . . but, in case you're interested, this is what I look like. ------------->

I do have a nose, by the way. I just don't feel like drawing it today.

OUT OF INTEREST, THOUGH, WHICH OF THESE NOSES DO YOU PREFER?

Ha ha! There you go again, picking your nose!

Anyway . . . when I told Mum about Janey
McVey she suggested I ask her to come for tea
at our house one night as a way of making her
feel part of our class. I said it was a good idea
in principle but that I'd have a think about it.

I'm thinking I'd much prefer to ask Layla.
She loves coming to our house for tea. Layla has
three little brothers (and her mum is
currently pregnant with **ANOTHER**
baby) so she often gets more
attention (and more BISCUITS)
at my house than when she's at
home. I love going to Layla's
house (especially when her mum's cooking goat
curry) — it's absolute BEDLAM.

Or, if Layla's busy, I could ask
Dale Redman, who, BTW, is my

DALE

hilarious (and often crazy) best **boy friend**.
I sit next to Dale for maths and English. It's a
good job we get along so well because Mrs
Patterson is OBSESSED with maths and English . . .

And yes, by the way, those two words up there
are separate: 'boy' and 'friend' not 'boyfriend'.
I'm **far too busy** for a boyfriend.

Patrick North and Daisy Muirhead say they are boyfriend and girlfriend. You wouldn't know it, though. They hardly ever speak to each other. Not like my sixteen-year-old cousin Tom and his girlfriend, Mia. They rarely speak to anyone else as their

faces are stuck together all the time: SNOGGING!

THIEF IN SCHOOL!

Today we were in the middle of practising our personal SPELLINGS (I wasn't showing Dale how to draw a bionic hand, honest) when we were all called into an unexpected SERIOUS ASSEMBLY by Mr Epping, our droney-onny head teacher.

Although assemblies are at the top of my mind-numbingly-boring-things-I'm-forced-to-do list, this one turned out to be seriously interesting.

BORING STUFF I'M FORCED TO DO
1. Assemblies
2. Supermarket shopping
3. Sitting quietly
4. School reading book
5. Practising SPELLINGS

The whole school traipsed into the hall and sat (uncomfortably) on the hard wooden floor. Everyone was whispering about what could possibly have caused Mr Epping to call an assembly at such an odd time (2.13 p.m.), and wondering what the 'serious' news might be.

Mr Bald Ball (who I suspect has a miniature head-sized version of his enormous mop) had even repolished the floor for the occasion

OUR CARETAKER

(which was good as it enabled Dale to break his bum-spin record: five full turns without stopping).

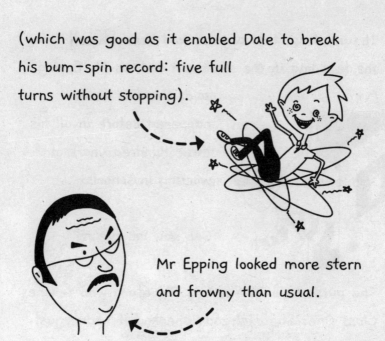

Mr Epping looked more stern and frowny than usual.

He called for **complete and utter** silence, then took a mega-deep breath and shook his head. 'Boys and girls,' he started, 'this is SERIOUS, very SERIOUS. I have something extremely SERIOUS to discuss with you.'

Can you tell from all those SERIOUSes how SERIOUS it was?

It turned out that a purse had been STOLEN from inside a bag in the staffroom and, as Mr Epping

said, this has never happened before in all his three hundred years of working in schools.

Can you believe it?

The purse belonged to Mrs Robinson, who teaches Class One. She'd already checked it hadn't just fallen out into her strange little old-lady car, conducted a thorough search of her classroom, and even been all the way home to check she hadn't left it on her kitchen table.

She looked extremely puffy-eyed and upset throughout the SERIOUS ASSEMBLY and I felt sorry for her because she's one of the really nice teachers.

Once, when I was in Class One, she let us colour in for so long that I melted a black crayon with my bare hand just from the pure effort of colouring in a witch's cape.

Anyway, Mr Epping said everyone was to have a 'long, hard think' about whether we knew where the purse was and, if anyone thought of anything that might be 'of interest', we should quietly go to his office and tell him. He also said if anyone was brave enough to own up to STEALING the purse, they'd be in far less trouble than if they let the matter 'FESTER'.

Since the SERIOUS ASSEMBLY, I've had a good think about the stolen purse and decided the thief

must have been Janey McVey — no one really knows a thing about her.

Or Liam Tabernacle from Class Six — he's always in trouble.

I will keep you updated on this SERIOUS matter.

TEN FAVE WORDS

1. spawn
2. skew-whiff
3. iridescent
4. indigo
5. wishy-washy
6. kerfuffle
7. ~~willy~~ fester
8. aquiver
9. topsy-turvy
10. boobs

PS I've added 'fester' to my ten favourite words list.

Sorry, 'willy', you've been cut. (Ouch!)

EXCLUSIVE CLUB

At school today Mrs Patterson asked Elliot Quinn how he'd figured out the answer to a tricky maths question and Elliot said (use your cleverest voice for this), 'I ADOPTED the long-multiplication method.'

ELLIOT

He meant he'd *used* long multiplication and he could have just said that (or that he'd timesed 698 by 465, or whatever the question was), but that's Elliot for you. He's like a mathematician and a walking dictionary. I like him. He's the perfect person to sit next to in tests . . .

Last year he taught me the longest word he knows (I dare you to try to say this):

floccinaucinihilipilification

Good try. It's actually pronounced:

floxi-norsi-ni-hilly-pill-iffy-kay-shun

I've no idea what it means, but I like the way it sounds. Anyway, I googled long words and came up with this:

pneumonoultramicroscopicsilicovolcanoconiosis

(It's some kind of lung disease.)

It has miles more letters than Elliot's daft word but I can't say it so I haven't told him yet. I have noticed, however, that it contains the word 'VOLCANO', which is pretty cool.

And, in case you thought you'd beaten me, **supercalifragilisticexpialidocious** doesn't count as that's a made-up word, and I could easily make up a longer one if that's allowed (which it's not but I will anyway).

Let's see . . .

boreyworeydroneyonnyextrawordynonsense

This word would be used to describe Mr Epping's way of talking in assemblies (unless a purse thief has struck and weirdly livened him up).

Anyway . . . when Elliot said the word 'ADOPTED', it made me remember something you might be interested in. I'm part of a very EXCLUSIVE club.

It's so EXCLUSIVE that (as far as I know) there are only three people in my school in it. You may join if you meet one vital condition: you must be ADOPTED.

I've not mentioned this so far as, honestly, I usually forget I'm ADOPTED. I know that might sound weird, but it's true. I simply don't have cause to think about it that much as, like you, I'm too busy getting on with life. But then someone will mention it to me (or use the word 'ADOPTED' for some other reason, like Elliot did today) and I suddenly remember.

OH YEAH!

It's not a big deal to me, though. It just makes me a bit different, and I like being different.

Like the time I styled my hair as a full-on bird's nest on Mad Hair Day — no one else did that.

No one was arrested for purse-stealing today, BTW. However, I still think Janey McVey is the culprit because she turned up for school wearing two EXTREMELY fancy hair scrunchies, which I suspect were bought with poor Mrs Robinson's STOLEN cash.

TODAY'S SPELLINGS

Nesisary?

Nessassary?

Necesury . . .

Needed . . .

Necessary.

Thanks, Mum . . . NECESSARY!

Sorry about that, Mum just came into my room.
She wasn't 100% pleased to find me wide awake
at almost 10 p.m. on a school night, but
she did mention how **delighted**
she was to see me practising
my SPELLINGS at home . . .

EEK!

She even rewarded me with
an extra-fancy new pen to go with my
STAY—AWAKE DOODLE DIARY so I guess
learning how to SPELL 'necessary' wasn't
a complete waste of time.

Mum kindly gave me a top tip that I'll share with you now:
'necessary' has one 'c' – like you only have one chin – and two 's's – like you have two socks.

Now I realize this won't be helpful to anyone reading who only has one leg but perhaps you could substitute socks for shoulders (unless you're doubly unlucky). Also, I've not got a clue how you remember all the other letters, but it's a start.

HOW DO I REMEMBER HOW TO SPELL 'NECESSARY'?

Unfortunately, Mum didn't leave me to it after sharing her half-good tip . . . She asked me what SPELLINGS we've been doing in class and what the chances of Mrs Patterson calling her in for another 'quiet word' might be . . .

I told her not to worry and that my wonderful SPELLINGS jotter was really helping me. Then to further put her off the this-is-not-actually-a-SPELLINGS-jotter scent (and possibly increase the chances of her buying me more fancy stationery) I mentioned how I'm considering becoming a dictionary writer when I'm older. That made her smiley.

stationEry

stationAry

I'm not, by the way. I think I'm going to be a scientist. Or a stuntwoman. Or a BISCUIT TESTER. But, if I was, I'd totally make sure all its words were spelled exactly as you say them to save all this nonsense.

In fact, I might draft another letter to the prime minister right now with my new fancy-pants (far too special for SPELLINGS) pen to suggest that the English language be given a complete overhaul.

Deer Pry Minister,
I hope U R OK. Pleez can U mayk a nyoo rool so evry1 has 2 spel wurds eggzacly the way they sownd? Thanks.
Luv,
Billie Upton Green x

PS Can U all-so mayk a lor banning peepul from corling eech uther by their inishuls?
PPS Wot did U think ov Layla's and my bisskit sujesschuns?

FRIDAY = FUNDAY

Layla and I love Fridays. It's Mrs Patterson's afternoon for putting her feet up in the staffroom drinking coffee, so Class Five has our favourite-ever teacher, Mrs Sharvane, instead.

Mrs Sharvane is AWESOME. She lets us sit wherever we want and often dishes out tiny chocolates for trying hard. She wears millions of rings (even on her thumbs) and always smells of fruit. Also, her eyes can change colour - one Friday they'll be green and the next they'll be blue. Pretty cool, hey?

Today she wore eight rings, her eyes were green, and she smelled of lemons.

Mrs Sharvane (who is almost as good as Mum at making up fabulous games that don't need any equipment) always lets us play a game towards the end of the day. She calls it Golden Time. I call it **'Yippee! Only half an hour until the weekend!'**

Today's game was called  THE STORY OF OLGA.

Basically Mrs Sharvane said a random statement about a woman called Olga and we took turns saying sentences about her, starting 'unluckily' or 'luckily'. It was supposed to remind us what a frontal lobe is or something.

It went like this . . .

MRS SHARVANE: One night Olga went out in her car to go to a music festival.

CORAL: Unluckily, halfway there, she ran out of petrol.

FARIDA: Luckily, a FAB-ulous petrol station was nearby.

FILL AND BEGONE

DAISY: Unluckily, the petrol station was closed.

CLOSED

ME: Luckily, Mrs Diesel, the owner of the petrol station, arrived to open up at that exact moment.

LAYLA: Unluckily, Mrs Diesel hadn't brought the keys to open the front door because she was pregnant, which made her terribly forgetful.

DOH!

JANEY: Luckily, Olga was a burglar in her spare time so she helped Mrs Diesel pick the lock with a long wire they found on the floor . . .

YOU'RE WELCOME.
FROM JMV, A
FELLOW THIEF

ELLIOT: Unluckily, Olga then realized she'd forgotten her purse so couldn't pay for any petrol.

DALE: Luckily, she found a ten-pound note in her bra . . .

TA-DA!!

You get the idea.

It was funny until Patrick North kept saying, 'Unluckily, then Olga died,' every time it got back round to him, and Mrs Sharvane wouldn't let us have people rising from the dead.

When I came out of school, Mum was in the yard chatting with someone I didn't recognize, but who looked super-stylish in long black boots and with her hair clipped fancily on top of her head.

I wondered if a MOVIE STAR was coming for tea.

MY DAUGHTER WOULD BE PERFECT FOR THE NEXT HOLLYWOOD BLOCKBUSTER.

No such luck. It turned out to be Mrs McVey, Janey's mum, and arrangements were being made for Janey to come to our house tomorrow.

I'd better lock up all my valuables . . .

JANEY = PAINY

Janey McVey is a **total** pain
in the actual leg. - - - - - - - - ➙

Before I tell you why, let me ask you
something: what are your parents like?

Well, I have two mums.

Now I know that might not be **your** usual but
it's **my** usual. I've had them since I was eight
months old. That's them up there, by the way.

In fact, I have two mums, two grandmas, one grandpa, one ~~aneshent~~ ~~ainshant~~ really old great-nan, who lives in a special home, a dog, three fish, nine cousins, seven aunties and five uncles. Beat that!

FINGERS

N-CHIPZ

PHILLY-O

If you have two mums like me, welcome to my even more EXCLUSIVE and mega-awesome club. If you've not got two mums, just think about how totally brilliant your one mum (or dad or granny or foster carer) is, then **double** it and you'll understand what I mean!

How many homes have you lived in? I've lived in THREE. Three homes and I'm only ten — now that's some going!

First I lived with my birth mother. In case you're wondering what that means (although I think it's pretty obvious), it means the lady who gave actual birth to me. My

BIRTH MUM'S HOUSE

birth mother's name is Wendy. She loved me and tried to look after me but found it too difficult. It wasn't my fault. She simply wasn't up to the job. Anyway, Wendy agreed it would be best if someone else became my parent. I don't remember a thing about my three weeks living with Wendy, but I do write to her every year and I know what she looks like. I might write more about Wendy on another day. I'll see how I'm feeling.

After that, I lived with some foster carers called Michael and Vickie. They took good care of me for a few months while an extra-clever social

FOSTER CARERS' HOUSE

worker looked for the perfect people to be my parents. I don't remember them either but Mums always say they were good people. I send them a Christmas card and a photo every year and they send my family one in return.

Now I live here with my FOREVER FAMILY! I think I'll live here forever, but when I'm a grown-up I might see if Stan and Shirley next door will sell me their house. I could knock a door through to my mums' house and we could still see each other every day.

FOREVER HOME

Anyway, I thought I'd tell you all that because I think I know you reasonably well now you've got to this page, and I have to say you seem nice and open-minded.

Mum says narrow-minded people sometimes take more time to get on with.

Well, when Janey McVey came round and discovered I had two mums she pulled up her nose. 'You can't have two mums,' she said.

None of my **real** friends have ever said that to me. They all know I have two mums. They've known it since reception class. It's NO BIG DEAL.

I said, 'Why not?'

She said, 'Because you have to have a dad.'

I said, 'No, you don't.'

She said, 'Which one is your real mum?'

I said, 'They're **both** my real mum.'

She said, 'That's impossible.'

As you can tell, as well
as being a THIEF, she's
not very clever either.

I said, 'If it's impossible,
how come I have two mums then? Did you think
one of them was made out of play dough?'

REAL MUM

PLAY-DOUGH
MUM

She said, 'Where's your dad?'

I said, 'Where's **your** dad?'

At that point Mum walked
into my bedroom and asked to
speak to me in another room in
her *I'm saying this quietly so I don't embarrass*
you, but I might be a little bit cross with you
voice.

Mum took me into the living room and said
I shouldn't be asking Janey about her dad as
her parents had recently divorced and it might
upset her.

I didn't tell Mum the whole lead-up to me
saying that. I decided to deal with Janey McVey
in my own way.

FACTS

So when I returned to my bedroom I told
Janey McVey the FACTS to put her straight.

'I'm ADOPTED, Janey,' I said.

'Oh, OK,' she said.

'Do you know what that means?' I asked her.
She nodded her head, but I decided to make
sure she wasn't faking. 'Go on then – what
does it mean?'

She shrugged her shoulders.

Just as I thought – I'm going to have to watch
this one closely. She's probably one of those
people who's seen a 'Please ADOPT this baby
tiger' advert on telly and then believes they
understand what ADOPTION is all about. Which

they don't — because 'ADOPTING' a tiger who lives millions of miles away is not real, actual ADOPTION. For that you merely send money every month, which the experts use to put towards a  tin of tiger food and, in return, send you a newsletter, which may or may not have a photo of your tiger in it and, if you're lucky, a cuddly toy. Real ADOPTION is not about money or newsletters or even cuddly toys. It's about LOVE — no matter what.

So I told Janey all about proper ADOPTION in a lot of detail.

'Oh, OK,' said Janey, picking up my new (too fancy for SPELLINGS) pen, no doubt wondering if she might be able to push it up her sleeve without me noticing. 'Shall we go and get a drink?'

Although I was also thirsty, I felt I should clear up the whole 'where's your dad?' thing before treating Janey to a glass of the special 'guests are coming over' fizzy orange I knew Mum had bought in preparation for her visit.

POP

ONLY OPEN
IF WE HAVE
GUESTS

So I told her how children can be ADOPTED by any adults (as long as they've passed some important tests to prove what awesome parents they'll be).

'Oh, OK,' said Janey.

'So not everyone has a mum and a dad,' I emphasized.

'Oh, OK,' said Janey.

Her oh-OKing was driving me mad by this point,
so I decided to finish my 'making Janey McVey
a little cleverer' session with a summary of the
main points, like Saleema does at the end of
every episode of *Saleema Selective: High-School
Detective* (#bestshowonTVfullstop).

'So,' I finished, 'both my mums ADOPTED me and
so they are **both** my **real** mums and I **don't**
have a dad and those are the FACTS.'

'OK, Billie,' she said. 'I get it. Shall we put some music on and make up a dance routine?'

I'm not sure she did get it fully – I think she was just desperate to show off again about being able to do the splits.

CIRCLE TIME RUINED

Mrs Patterson is a bit of a battleaxe. 'Firm but fair,' Mum says.

FIRM STANCE

FAIR HAIR

By the way, I always just say 'Mum' as you might have noticed. And what I'm thinking is you don't know which one I'm talking about, even though I definitely do.

My mums are called Katie and Sarah and they always say they don't mind what I call them. (Although I'm not sure

KATIE

SARAH

how they'd feel if I called them POTATO and LAMPSHADE – which, of course, I never would . . .)

When I was little, I used to call Katie 'Mum' and Sarah 'Mummy'. But I've stopped saying 'Mummy' in public as Patrick North once heard me and said I sounded babyish. I don't usually agree with a single word Patrick North says, but I kind of agreed with that one time. So now I just call them both 'Mum'. It's handy, really, because if I yell 'MUM!' both of them reply 'YES?' and I have **double** the attention!

Occasionally I call them 'Mum K' and 'Mum S', but only if I really need a specific mum. Like, if I need something fixing, I'll **always** call for Mum K because Mum S is sooo bad at fixing problems. (As I've discovered on many unfortunate occasions . . .)

ITEM	HOW IT SHOULD LOOK	THE PROBLEM	RESULT AFTER GETTING MUM S TO HELP
GOGGLES			
BIKE			
KNICKER DRAWER			

Or if I'm in the mood for baking, I ALWAYS
shout for Mum S as Mum K refuses
to bake anything that doesn't
involve an assortment of random

CARROT AND
SWEDE MUFFINS

CUCUMBER
MUSH CAKES

vegetables . . .

Whereas Mum S bakes
proper cakes – like
chocolate bums.

BEETROOT
SURPRISE

And, yes, they are called
chocolate **BUMS**, not buNs in
case you were thinking (understandably) I'd
made a SPELLING mistake. See why?!

CHOCOLATE
(NOT POO)

They've told me I can use 'Katie' and 'Sarah' if
I want to, but I like saying 'mum'. It suits me.

Anyway . . . what was I talking about? Oh yes,
Mrs Patterson . . .

She's hard work sometimes. Like today in circle
time she asked us all to think of something nice
about Janey McVey and say it aloud to her so
she'd feel welcome and happy in our class.
I was halfway round the circle, which was good
as it gave me some much-needed thinking time.

Patrick North was first. He said,
'Janey has nice hair.'

I suppose that's true, if you like
fancy (possibly bought
with STOLEN cash)
scrunchies and too many clips.

HOW CAN I
INCORPORATE THE
WORD 'FAB' INTO
THIS . . .?

Then Farida Banerjee went
on and on about how Janey
was a FAB-ulous PE partner.

I have no EVIDENCE to either confirm or deny this as I'm ALWAYS partners with Layla.

Layla was next. She said Janey was funny when she told jokes in the yard. I wondered where I'd been when this happened as I've **never** heard Janey tell a joke. I suddenly felt desperate to interrupt and remind Layla how awesome my jokes are by telling her the one I heard on the radio this morning, but in circle time we are STRICTLY FORBIDDEN from talking unless we're holding the SPECIAL CUP.

ACTUALLY JUST A BLUE BEAKER WITH A BIT OF TINSEL ON ITS RIM

Obviously I'm not holding the blue beaker right now under my covers, but I will interrupt myself to share my joke with you:

Why did the toilet roll jump off the tall building?

TO QUICKLY GET TO THE BOTTOM!!

Elliot described in great detail how Janey had taught him a good method for remembering 7 x 8 = 56.

My good friend Coral Munro said Janey was good
at doing the splits (which was an extra-kind
thing to say about someone who'd obviously been
showing off).

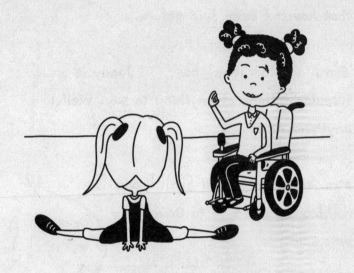

And so it went on and, before I knew it, it was
my turn and I hadn't thought
of anything.

'Come on, Billie,' said
Mrs Patterson. 'Today!'

'Erm, erm, Janey has nice hair?' I suggested.

'Yes, Billie, but Patrick has already said that, and I'd rather we tried to come up with things that haven't been said before.'

'Erm,' I said. 'Janey has . . . Janey is . . .' I couldn't think of anything to say. Well, anything nice.

Mrs Patterson got all STRICT and LOUD and moved on to Dale, who said:

CAN I GO TO THE TOILET?!

So now Janey McVey is a THIEF, she's a bit dim about real life, and she's got me in trouble. I AM NOT PLEASED.

AMAZING ANNOUNCEMENT

OMG and OMG, do I have some news to share! This afternoon, after we'd taken Mr Paws for a stroll (he's our dog, by the way — we don't take random men out for walks) . . .

. . . I was about to settle down to watch a few episodes of *Saleema Selective: High-School Detective* when, out of the blue, Mums announced we were going out for a special dinner.

Put on something nice — we're going out for dinner!

Despite it being no one's birthday, both my grandmas and my grandpa met us at the restaurant, so I knew something was AFOOT.

I like the word 'afoot'. Not quite enough to add it to my favourite words list but it would probably rank at number eleven.
It basically means 'about to happen'.

A FOOT

It was an **extremely** fancy place. We had two forks and two knives each, and the waiter who was in charge of serving our table actually put our napkins (which were like cute mini tablecloths) on our knees for us!

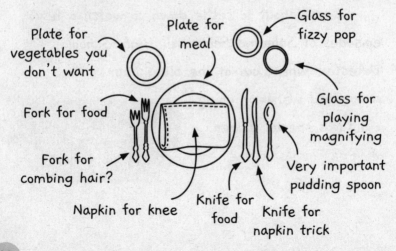

Plate for vegetables you don't want

Plate for meal

Glass for fizzy pop

Fork for food

Glass for playing magnifying

Fork for combing hair?

Very important pudding spoon

Napkin for knee

Knife for food

Knife for napkin trick

Anyway, after pudding (I had hot chocolate fudge cake with ice cream) Mum K started tapping her glass with the fork she hadn't used. I thought she wanted to play Join In With a Rhythm, which is one of our favourite mealtime games, so I quickly guzzled the last of my fizzy orange and began banging out a beat with my glass on the table. It turned out, however, that Mum was doing the funny fork-on-glass tapping to get everyone to be quiet.

OOPS!

THIS MEANS BE QUIET

Anyway . . . then Mum K looked at Mum S, who was looking all sunny and happy (I also suspect she was a bit tipsy – which means she had drunk a glass of wine) and said they had some REALLY SPECIAL news to share.

Mum K was acting a lot like I do when it's time for show-and-tell and I have something extra interesting to share that I know Mrs Patterson won't be able to dismiss as un-newsworthy – like the time Patrick North announced he'd got a new toothbrush . . .

AND YOU'LL NEVER GUESS WHAT. IT'S BLUE, NOT RED!

Guess what the news was!

A. We're getting a new car with TVs in the back of the seats.

B. We're going to Disneyland.

C. We're getting our loft converted into a cinema.

Answer: NONE OF THE ABOVE! (Although all will be immediately added to my wish list.)

WISH LIST

1. Go to Iceland (the country, not the shop)
2. Visit London (to discuss BISCUITS with Law Makers)
3. Get a new bike (with gears)
4. Make vegetables UNHEALTHY and sweets healthy
5. Get Mum to buy better crisps

The news was: my mums are finally getting MARRIED! And **even better** . . .

I'm going
to be a
BRIDESMAID!

YIPPPEEEE! I've always wanted to be a BRIDESMAID!

Grandma Jude and Grandpa (whose name is Ted, by the way; I just call him Grandpa as he's the only one I have because sadly Mum K's dad is dead) were all talkative and smiley and question-asky. Granny Pauline cried uncontrollably because she was, as she kept saying, 'so over the moon' (not because she hates weddings).

It's a bit annoying the wedding isn't going to happen next weekend as I know I'm free but, on the positive side, I now have plenty of time to think of who to invite, what to wear, what music I'd like to dance to, and what I'd like to say!

I've only ever been to one wedding before – it was Uncle Andrew and Aunty Sal's – but I was only two and I can't remember it. I've seen the video, though, and my favourite part was when

I yelled 'I need a poo, Mummy!' right in the middle of an important talky bit. It made everyone laugh, which was good as no one was laughing at the l . . . o . . . n . . . g, dull speech.

YADA . . . YADA . . . YADA . . .

I NEED A POO!

I'm so excited I'm not sure if I'll be able to sleep at all this week, never mind tonight. When I said this to Mum earlier, she suggested I make a list of everything on my mind. (I also think being tipsy had made her sleepy and not in the mood for a lengthy chat at eleven o'clock at night.)

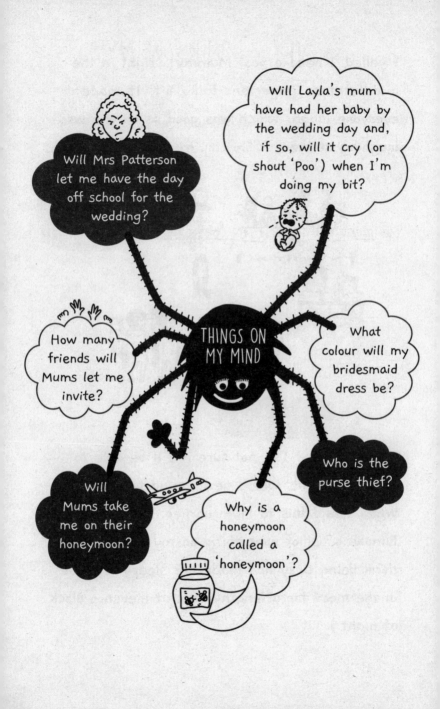

JANEY = VERY PAINY

Layla was so excited by my news! Much more excited than when she'd told me about her mum expecting 'YET ANOTHER' baby.

We played BRIDESMAIDS in the playground and got loads of people to join in.

I was the BRIDESMAID when Elliot married Layla. Then Layla was the BRIDESMAID when I married Dale. Then Elliot was the BRIDESMAID when Dale married Layla, and then Janey McVey came over and asked us what we were doing.

Layla told her we were playing Weddings and asked her if she wanted to join in. She said she did.

So she was the BRIDESMAID while I married Elliot. Then I was the BRIDESMAID while she married Dale. Then Dale complained he hadn't been the BRIDESMAID, so Layla said he could be the BRIDESMAID while she married Janey.

Janey looked at Layla and laughed. 'Two girls can't get married,' she said.

She really is going to have to get up to date with how things are.

Layla said, 'Yes, they can. Billie's mums are getting married.'

'Who to?' asked Janey.

'To each other, you cuckoo,' said Elliot.

CUCKOO CLOCK

'Oh, OK,' said Janey McVey.

I mean, I know we all have to learn new facts every now and then, and not everyone picks things up as quickly as me, but Janey seems to know NOTHING about life.

NOTHING TO SEE HERE

'Of course two girls can get married,' I said, 'and before you tell Elliot he can't marry Dale, two boys can get married in real life too, you know.'

'Really?!' exclaimed Janey.

'Yes,' I said.

'It's true,' added Dale. 'My next-door-but-one neighbours are both boys and they're married to each other.'

'Oh, OK,' she said (AGAIN!), before turning to smirk at me as though she may have actually known this FACT already.

Anyway, a few seconds later Mrs Patterson blasted her whistle and for once I was glad to have to immediately 'STAND STILL AND BE SILENT' because having to keep telling Janey McVey facts everyone should know is getting terribly tiresome.

In the afternoon Elliot advised me not to get frustrated with Janey. 'Maybe she's just never encountered anyone who falls outside usual stereotypes,' he said.

According to Elliot, a 'stereotype' is what people imagine straight away when you say something. Like, if I said, 'My cousin is football-mad,' you might imagine: ------>

But my cousin might actually look like this:

Although a stereotyper isn't something I EVER plan to become, I do think it's an interesting word. So much so that it's made it on to my list. This time I'm cutting 'boobs' (ouch again).

TEN FAVE WORDS

1. spawn
2. skew-whiff
3. iridescent
4. indigo
5. wishy-washy
6. kerfuffle
7. ~~willy~~ fester
8. aquiver
9. topsy-turvy
10. ~~boobs~~ stereotype

I didn't let Janey's (possibly fake) dimness stop me sharing my news at show-and-tell time.

Everyone clapped and Mrs Patterson said she thought I'd make a 'wonderful and beautiful' BRIDESMAID. She even allowed people to ask questions. Janey asked me what colour my BRIDESMAID dress was going to be. I informed her I have a meeting with my designer soon, which, if Grandma Jude is going to make it, is not a lie.

Anyway, guess what Janey said . . .

OH, OK.

DETECTIVE WORK

Today everyone was interviewed by Mr Epping about Mrs Robinson's stolen purse.

It was scary. We had to line up a class at a time and then go into his office for a little chat.

When Layla came out, she looked awful. It made me wonder if Mr Epping was force-feeding pupils pieces of Turkish delight to extract confessions. Turkish delight, BTW, is one of my and Layla's joint hates. We NEVER eat anything made of shampoo.

When it was my turn, Mr Epping said:

HELLO, BILLIE, HOW ARE YOU TODAY?

HEADTEACHER

So I told him about my verruca, and that my torch needs new batteries, and how my breakfast had made me feel extremely full (because 'I'm all right' always seems like a dull answer to such an open question).

Mr Epping told me he'd noticed that I was good at spotting things and asked if I knew anything about Mrs Robinson's purse going missing.

'I have a couple of theories,' I began, looking around his office for his beloved shampoo-flavoured confectionery. (I didn't spot any.)

He asked me if my theories were based on FACT.

I said, 'Kind of fact and kind of just knowing how certain people are.'

When I told him my suspicions – about Janey McVey and Liam Tabernacle – he shook his head and said I shouldn't accuse people without HARD FACTS. He did ask me, however, to keep my 'ear to the ground', which I know means listen out for clues in case I find out any useful information I can pass on.

So I've decided to do a bit of detective work –
when I can fit it in.

Actually I have a little time right now . . .

Top ten suspects for the
stolen-purse situation:

1. JANEY MCVEY – you know why.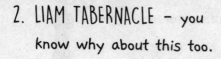

2. LIAM TABERNACLE – you
   know why about this too.

3. MR ~~BALD~~ BALL - I've
noticed he always wears
trousers with about 168
pockets, so he definitely
has plenty of places to
hide STOLEN goods. Also,
nobody supervises him

PURSE?

HEAD-SHINER

and his giant mop. He could easily have
slipped into the staffroom when everyone else
was doing silent reading (or, as I like to call
it, silent-ish daydreaming).

4. DAISY MUIRHEAD - she goes to the toilet
more often than anyone I've ever known in
my whole life. Mum says she must have
some problems with her piping
'down there', by which she
means her bladder. But maybe
Daisy goes out of class for a
nosy around every half hour to
see if she can find anything
to STEAL.

5. A RANDOM THIEF flounced into school, nabbed the purse and sauntered out without anyone noticing. Although this is unlikely (as Miss Woods, our super-strict school secretary with melon-sized muscles, guards the front door like a Rottweiler), it's not impossible. What if Miss Woods was holding an important meeting about registers or dinner money, and had left the front door unlocked?

6. MRS TRAPP – our head dinner lady. She's horrible – so she certainly has the potential to be a THIEF. She once forced me to eat a strip of steamed cabbage and half a floret of broccoli and I puked on my plate a few seconds later. OK, that's a bit of an exaggeration, but I did get into trouble for doing the loudest burp ever that afternoon.

7. CALEB – the guy who comes into school to fix dodgy smartboards and broken laptops. He's constantly wandering between classrooms fiddling with our stuff, often when we're all in assembly. Loads of girls say they're in love with Caleb and go on about how handsome he is but, as I know very well, you shouldn't judge people on their appearance. Handsome people can be thieves too.

8. JANEY MCVEY – deserves another mention so you don't forget.

9. MRS ROBINSON *might* have made a mistake. She is about ninety-three years old and I know old people can forget things. My great-nan once forgot how old she was. No jokes.

10. JANEY MCVEY.

WEDDING PLANNING

We went to choose a venue for BRIDESMAID DAY today.

I was mega interested and excited at first but that soon wore off. Basically we spent YONKS in the car being yelled at (and lied to) by Mrs Satnav, looked at about ninety-seven big empty rooms, and read a GAZILLION 'wedding breakfast' menus.

'Wedding breakfast', by the way, is the official name for the fancy three-course meal everyone enjoys after a wedding ceremony. I have no idea why they keep calling it a breakfast as:

a) cereal did not feature on any of the menus, and

b) the wedding is going to be on a Saturday **afternoon**.

NOT A WEDDING BREAKFAST

Anyway, after about three years, Mums EVENTUALLY made a decision.

Annoyingly, they chose the first one we'd been to see (so missing this afternoon's double episode of *Saleema Selective: High-School Detective* was completely ~~unnecissary~~ ~~unnecassary~~ pointless).

Splendidly, their choice was also my favourite because:

1. The chef told me he would make me an EXTRAORDINARY Eton mess (for breakfast pudding).

2. The dance floor was extra shiny (PERFECT for sock skids).

3. It had a pool (handy if we fancy a quick dip after all the BRIDESMAIDY activities).

So, exciting news, BRIDESMAID DAY will be held at Manor Grove Hotel and Spa.

A 'spa' is not, by the way, the same as a Spar . . . At a spa you can get a massage and maybe have your toenails painted. At a Spar you can pick up a loaf of bread and try to win a million pounds by buying a scratch card (which we are NEVER allowed to do).

'ELLO, 'ELLO, 'ELLO

You'll never guess what . . .

A POLICE OFFICER came into assembly today - a real-life, official police officer on official, genuine police business. It totally spiced up morning droning.

She said she wanted to talk to us about behaviour choices . . .

First she asked us to put up our hands if we thought we knew right from wrong and could give an example. Loads of people are shy about putting up their hands in assembly in case their answer gets laughed at. I'm not. I was the first with my hand up.

'It is **right** to chew with your mouth closed and **wrong** to open your mouth when you're eating.'

I said this because I was sitting next to Patrick North, who seriously needs to learn this basic fact. If Grandma Jude saw him eating, she'd 100% say, **'His table manners leave a lot to be desired.'**

Dale was next to be addressed and he said, 'It is right to support Man U and not right to support Chelsea.' Everyone laughed – even the police officer until Mr Epping glared at her from over his little half-moon glasses.

NO LAUGHING MATTER!

95

'But what about *doing* the right thing?' the police lady said when all the giggling had died down. 'I've heard *someone* at this school might have done something very wrong. And I'm not talking about forgetting your homework.'

Janey McVey raised her hand. 'It is wrong to steal,' she said solemnly.

Mr Epping beamed at her proudly and the police lady gave her lots of praise before lecturing us on how wrong stealing is and why it's wrong and blah, blah, blah . . . but I kept my eye on Janey McVey. She looked a little too smug for my liking.

So, at dinner break I left Layla trying to finish Mrs Trapp's awful 'cat-sick pie' and conducted my own little interview with Janey.

THURSDAY SPECIAL

Unfortunately, she was playing hopscotch with Patrick North and Farida Banerjee.

TERRIBLE TRIO

'May I join in?' I asked.

'Sure, Billie,' said Janey, all innocent and nice.

'As long as you don't start BUG-ing us,' said Patrick, grinning.

Farida laughed.

I decided to ignore Patrick's disregard for my number-one rule in the interests of THIEF CATCHING. 'Can you remember your first day at this school, Janey?' I enquired casually.

She said she could and that, although she'd been nervous, we'd all made her feel welcome.

'What about your second day? Can you remember that?' I continued.

Janey started going on about how she'd enjoyed coming to my house (which wasn't even on her second day) and how nice my mums are (true but irrelevant), so I interrupted her attempts to make me like her (and possibly steer me away from gaining HARD—FACT proof that she's the purse THIEF) by saying, 'What about when you **were actually at school** on your SECOND day? Can you remember anything in particular about that?'

'Er, maybe,' she said.

I took that 'er' to mean she was about to tell a lie.

'It's your turn, Billie,' said Farida, her hands on her hips.

I threw my stone to number one and slowly scotched and hopped up and down while thinking about which way to take my questioning.

'It was the day Mrs Robinson's purse was STOLEN,' I said when I got back to number one and picked up my stone.

'Oh yes,' she said. 'What about it?'

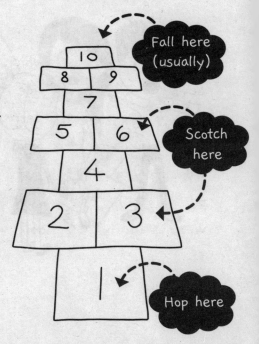

Fall here (usually)

Scotch here

Hop here

'Did you go to the toilet that day?'

'What are you talking about, Bug?' said Patrick. 'Of course she did. She's not a robot, you know.'

At that point Liam Tabernacle's football came hurtling towards us.

I've not a clue how Janey didn't see it coming, but I suspect she stepped into its path completely on purpose to bring my carefully planned interview to an abrupt end.

SHE'S ON TO ME.

I MUST GO INSIDE FOR A WET PAPER TOWEL IMMEDIATELY.

INVITATIONS

I helped Mums make a guest list for the wedding this evening.

Planning a wedding guest list takes FOREVER – mainly because you have to make a million decisions like:

1. Who you **want** to invite.
2. Who you **have** to invite (because they are related to you).
3. Who you **can't** invite (because they don't get along with someone you **have** to invite).
4. Who might be special enough to attend the **whole thing**.
5. Who might be invited to the **evening 'do' only** – a night-time disco that about one hundred people can attend. (OMG, BRIDESMAID DAY is going to be so awesome!)

6. Whether you will put 'plus one' - like this, '+1' - on the invitations you give to people you're not confident will come on their own. (Why you would leave out your 101st best friend just so a randomer can tag along with Shy Sheila from work, I don't know.)

7. Whether you should tell people to bring presents or not, or even tell them *exactly* what present to buy you, which in my opinion sounds rather cheeky (but also rather splendid).

When I plan a guest list for a birthday party, I have to:

1. Pick my favourite friends and give them an invitation.

LAYLA
DALE
ELLIOT
CORAL

Anyway, after I'd added Layla and Dale to the whole-thing list in capital letters, I left Mums to it in favour of a quick catch-up with *Saleema Selective: High-School Detective*.

This was a HUGE mistake.

When I wandered back into the kitchen, the list was almost complete and I immediately noticed three things.

EXCELLENT THING: Layla was still on the whole-thing list and her whole family had been added too.

DISAPPOINTING-BUT-NOT-TOO-BAD THING:
Dale and his grandad had been demoted to
the evening-do-only list.

ABSOLUTELY TERRIBLE THING: Janey and her
mum and '+1' had been added to the evening-do-
only list.

'**WHAT? WHY?**' I shouted.

And that's when Mum S informed me that Janey's
mum had recently joined her art class and they'd
become friends. According to Mum, Mrs Nicole
McVey is a 'warm-hearted, interesting woman'.

'Janey must take after her dad then,' I huffed.

This led to Mum telling me off for being
~~unnecissary~~ ~~unnecessery~~ unnecessary - which is
what she says when she thinks I might be saying
something a teeny-weeny bit mean.

So I told Mums about Janey McVey not even knowing that two women or two men can get married to each other until very recently. This caused them to glance at each other as though they didn't believe me. 'Well, everyone has to learn things for the first time at some point, Billie,' said Mum S.

When I left the room, I heard Mum K saying something like, 'Nicole's obviously chosen to shield Janey from her hair's antics then!'

I could be mistaken about the 'her hair's' bit (as Mum K went extra quiet at this point), so I'm still trying to work out what she meant.

PS Mums said they are both wearing white dresses, so I can choose any colour for mine. At the moment I'm thinking black because I like things to CONTRAST.

PPS Whoa! Mr Paws has just done THE STINKIEST trump . . .

EXPERIMENTING

Janey McVey is 100% a THIEF and here's my HARD—FACT proof . . .

In science this afternoon Mrs Patterson put us into pairs and announced we were doing 'an exciting experiment'.

Unfortunately, Mrs Patterson's idea of 'an exciting experiment' is **completely** different from mine. I mean, who doesn't know what happens to water if you add blue food colouring or red paint or a green felt-tip without its lid? Yawnarama.

USING <u>ONLY</u> THE EQUIPMENT PROVIDED, MAKE YOUR BEAKERS OF WATER CHANGE COLOUR.

Fortunately, I was with Dale, who was easily persuaded to veer away from Mrs Patterson's guidelines ever so slightly, enabling us to be actual scientists.

Well, when Janey McVey slunk over to us (probably aiming to STEAL our amazing ideas) she totally got all jealous and telltaley.

'Mrs Patterson . . .' she blabbed. 'Billie and Dale are not following your instructions.'

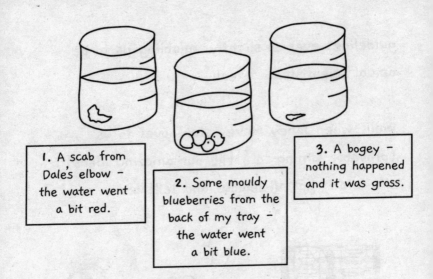

1. A scab from Dale's elbow – the water went a bit red.

2. Some mouldy blueberries from the back of my tray – the water went a bit blue.

3. A bogey – nothing happened and it was gross.

To cut a long (and quite shouty) story short, Mrs Patterson made me and Dale stay inside for the whole of playtime, and Janey smirked at us on her way out.

I usually enjoy science but this 'changes' topic is turning out to be the dullest thing ever. I'm hoping Mrs Patterson might consider switching it to 'inventing crumbless BISCUITS' soon. I'm not holding my breath, though, because when I suggested this well-thought-out idea to her she shushed me quite loudly and told me to get on with my punishment (copying out a paragraph about how somebody really boring once did a quite boring thing with a fairly boring bit of mould).

So, there you go – PROOF. Janey basically STOLE my afternoon break by being a great big telltale. I'm not sure it'll be enough to satisfy Mr Epping, but my EVIDENCE is slowly building up.

EVIDENCE
1. Being new and unknown
2. New scrunchies the day after the purse went missing
3. Looking smug
4. Getting bonked on the head with a ball on purpose to avoid answering questions
5. Stealing my playtime

(NOT) NICES

Alarmingly, Mum S agreed with Janey McVey's mum that I would go to her house for tea today. Why she didn't run this by me, I don't know. It was a good job I didn't have plans to go snowboarding or begin learning to play the harp or anything. Hmph. Anyway, lucky for Mum, I realized I was free when she suggested I could always make a start on learning my seven times tables instead, so I went.

LET ME JUST CHECK MY SCHEDULE.

Here's what I discovered during two hours in the company of a potential purse THIEF and her fancy-looking mum:

1. Janey and her mum live in a small flat. The way Janey talks I'd imagined she lived in some kind of grand mansion with scrunchie-applicator servants and a splits-practising ballroom.

2. Janey's middle name is Annabel. I told her if we were still using initials as nicknames (which we are definitely not) she'd be called Jam, which isn't too bad.

3. Janey has no pets, not even a fish.

4. Janey's mum is a skilful cook. For tea we had beans and egg on delicious extra-buttery thick white toast.

5. I **DO NOT** like Nice BISCUITS. In fact, I believe Layla and I need to make a new law for the disgusting coconutty rectangles Janey's mum tried to pass off as a tasty snack . . .

NICE

NASTY

BISCUIT LAW 6:
Avoid at all costs

6. Despite having a quick nosy around while we were playing hide-and-seek, I found no sign of an old lady purse lurking about the place, so unfortunately I'm no nearer to being able to present Mr Epping with any HARD EVIDENCE. Chances are, however, the THIEF, whoever it may be, has thrown the purse away and spent the cash (possibly on scrunchies).

7. Janey is obsessed with pens. She had a pot with about a million weird and wonderful

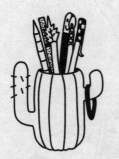 ballpoints on her bedroom windowsill.

OMG, I've just realized, I've not seen my extra-fancy important SPELLING-practice pen since Janey was fiddling about with it in my bedroom . . .

GREAT-NAN

We went to visit my great-nan after tea this evening.

Great-Nan is Granny Pauline's mum. She has false teeth, extra-wobbly legs and terrible wind.

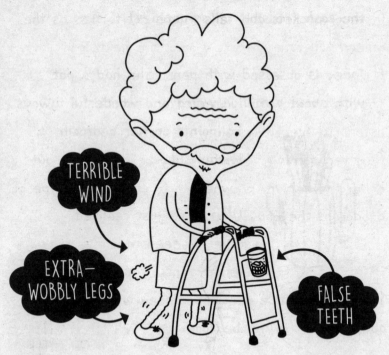

TERRIBLE
WIND

EXTRA-
WOBBLY LEGS

FALSE
TEETH

Until last year Great-Nan lived with Granny P.

Now she lives in a special overheated home that was invented for old people who like watching TV on MAX VOLUME with their eyes closed.

Great-Nan used to save all her extra-shiny pennies and 2ps for me to spend on sweets. Now she gives me tubes of toothpaste and little bars of soap in waxy packets and tells Mums not to fuss as the nurses will bring her new ones the next day.

The best thing about Great-Nan is that she always listens to everything I say. (A lot of adults pretend they're listening but often they're thinking about doing the laundry or whether to change the type of deodorant they buy.)

I MUST REMEMBER TO IRON MY KNICKERS . . .

MUM, MUM, I NEED THIS NEW GAME FOR MY COMPUTER.

So she was terribly excited when I told her all about BRIDESMAID DAY.

'I'll see if I'm free,' she said. 'Fetch my diary.'

Apart from '**remember to take my pills**' written on every single page, her diary was otherwise blank, so I think she'll be able to make it.

After a while of Great-Nan telling us about her false teeth and crazy-sounding friends, Mums suggested I might like to nip down to the games room to entertain myself. This would have been impossible as the games room consists of a table, seven dusty jigsaw puzzles and a box of dominoes. However, I did discover a storeroom full of ZIMMER frames on my way there, so I entertained myself with those instead.

That was fun until a nurse told me off so loudly that Mum heard and came dashing to investigate the commotion . . .

Zimmer – it's a pretty cool word, don't you agree? In fact, yes, I like it even better than

Although the special-home corridors pong of wee, Great-Nan says she likes living there with all her friends.

TEN FAVE WORDS
1. spawn
2. skew-whiff
3. iridescent
4. indigo
5. wishy-washy
6. kerfuffle
7. ~~willy~~ fester
8. ~~aquiver~~ Zimmer
9. topsy-turvy
10. ~~boobs~~ stereotype

Apparently she gets a three-course meal every night, and today a lady had pushed her in a wheelchair to the TV room and painted her nails for her. It's a bit like a spa, I suppose.

#BFF

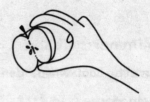

After we'd shared our (equally disappointing) snacks this morning, Layla and I made a start on rehearsing the dance routine we've decided will form a major part of BRIDESMAID DAY.

At the moment it involves a lot of stepping back and forth, putting our arms up and down, a bit of twirling and some shimmying. But we have plans to include an impressive lift at the end (if Layla can quickly get a bit stronger and make fewer heaving noises).

Unfortunately, Janey McVey kept disturbing us — offering to teach us how to do the splits to

make the dance more professional.
Layla looked surprisingly
tempted by that idea, so
I called an early end to
the rehearsal and suggested
we play Opposites
instead.

'Do you really want to?'
asked Layla.

'No!' I said (because you can't catch me out
that easily).

'OK,' said Layla. 'What colour
are your shoes?'

I said, 'White,' then asked
her whether the sky is
up or down.

WHITE

She said, 'Down,' then asked me what my
favourite BISCUIT is.

I said, 'Nice BISCUITS – have you had one yet?'

She said, 'No, they're NICE!' and we both burst
out laughing.

'Can I talk to you in private, Layla?' interrupted
Janey.

Layla glanced at me. Then she looked at Janey
and said, 'Yes, sure!' and she wasn't being
opposite . . .

I was left gobsmacked and watched them walk off
to the big tree together.

In the cloakroom I asked Layla what Janey
had wanted. Apparently my mention of
Nice BISCUITS had reminded Janey
of her dad and she'd confided in
Layla about how upset it makes
her that she's not seeing
him very often.

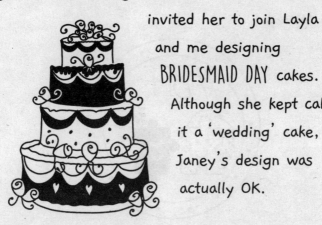

I felt a bit sorry for
Janey then because I
know her mum doesn't have
a car and I expect it's too far to walk 356 miles
just for a dad hug. So at wet dinner break I
invited her to join Layla
and me designing
BRIDESMAID DAY cakes.
Although she kept calling
it a 'wedding' cake,
Janey's design was
actually OK.

Before Janey left us
to play hangman with
Patrick North, she
mentioned she was
going to ask her mum
if Layla could go over for
tea soon. 'Well, you've
already been, Billie,' she
added.

I spent the rest of dinner break making Layla
a BEST FRIEND badge - so she doesn't forget
and accidentally become BEST FRIENDS with
Janey McVey.

HEDGEHOGS

Me and Layla were having a quietish chat about the purse thief and wondering when she/he will strike again when Mrs Sharvane interrupted us to tell me she'd seen me at Great-Nan's special home the other evening.

'Why didn't you shout hello or something, Mrs Sharvane?' I asked.

She said, 'You were in the middle of being told off for messing about in a cupboard full of Zimmer frames.'

'Oh,' I said.

To change the subject, I asked Mrs Sharvane if *she* had any thoughts about the purse THIEF.

'I think Mr Epping has let the matter go,' she said. 'Get on with your work and stop chatting.'

This left me and Layla confused for two reasons:

CONFUSED EYES

1. Mr Epping NEVER 'lets things go'.
2. Mrs Sharvane NEVER says 'stop chatting'.

At break time Layla and I decided we definitely
need to bring the matter up with Mr Epping and
certainly before next week as, in assembly this
morning, he instructed everyone to bring in some
money next week to donate to hedgehogs.

Save the Hedgehogs is the charity our school is
supporting this year,
BTW. I've no idea
what the hedgehogs
need money for, but
if the THIEF got wind
of millions of extra
pounds arriving in everyone's book bags, they
could get ideas.

HOGS R US!

SPIKE FILES

50% SALE

When Janey McVey came over and asked what we were talking about, I blurted out 'Pets!' as I still have my suspicions about Janey. Janey said she wished she had a dog. I told her she could come and see Mr Paws sometime, but not this weekend as I have plans. Which I don't. But I'm going to ask Mum if Layla can come round.

I've no idea *why* Mrs Sharvane was at Great-Nan's special home, by the way – I've just realized I forgot to ask her. I think I must have been too distracted by her peach-scented hair, and a bit annoyed she gave her 'tiny chocolate award' to Patrick North just because he'd finally managed to draw a person with a neck.

DALE

Mums said I could invite Layla
over for the **whole day!**

BUT . . .

When I rang the Dixon house, Layla's mum
said Layla was at Janey
McVey's flat and
would be there
until teatime . . .

I think Layla must have lost the badge I
made her . . .

Instead of all the amazing activities I had
planned to do with my #BFF, I ended up going
to a boring old garden centre to look at plants
and flowers that Mums might have at their
wedding. Apart from a new addition to my ten

favourite words list, it was all rather yawnsome until we bumped into Dale and his grandad.

Dale was darting up and down the outdoor aisles and his grandad was chasing him.

TEN FAVE WORDS

1. spawn
2. skew-whiff
3. iridescent
4. indigo
5. wishy-washy
6. kerfuffle
7. ~~willy~~ fester
8. ~~aquiver~~ Zimmer
9. ~~topsy-turvy~~ delphinium
10. ~~boobs~~ stereotype

It looked like a pretty cool game.

CATCH ME IF YOU CAN!

SLOW DOWN, DALE. YOU'LL CAUSE AN ACCIDENT!

Anyway, after a bit of chatting, Mum asked Dale's grandad if he'd like Dale to come to our house for a couple of hours. He did. So Dale came and it was lots of fun.

We played COPS AND ROBBERS. Dale was an American cop. He wore Mum's sunglasses and found a water pistol to use as his gun. I played a robber from 356 miles away called Painy McVoo. Mr Paws was a poor old lady from Paris called Mrs Robindaughter who'd had her purse stolen,

STICK 'EM UP.

and then her wig, and then her false teeth, and then her Zimmer frame.

After that, Mum suggested we have a bit of quiet time, so we went downstairs to watch *Saleema Selective: High-School Detective* with a drink and a BISCUIT.

That's when Dale broke the law . . .

BISCUIT LAW number one, to be precise. He gobbled a Bourbon in two single bites!

OMG

I realized it was a matter of great importance to properly demonstrate all the serious BISCUIT LAWS to Dale to reduce his risk of future imprisonment. (Well, the prime minister is obviously taking them seriously, otherwise we'd have received a 'sorry, no' reply by now.) Mum didn't sound too sure but when Dale suggested we play CURTAIN-CLIMB instead, she surrendered, allowing us to quietly gorge on an assortment of BISCUITS until Dale's grandad came to collect him. RESULT!

Dale lives with his grandad, BTW. He does see his mum sometimes on Wednesdays after school but she often drinks too much wine – that's why he can't live with her. Dale says he likes it this way because his grandad is super fun whereas his mum is often sad. My mums are usually happy like me. Apart from when they find out I've been messing with Zimmer frames – then they tell me they are 'sad' about my behaviour. (OMG, imagine if they discovered this 'SAD' Diary!)

WE'RE VERY SAD ABOUT THIS SAD BEHAVIOUR, BILLIE.

Also, they only drink wine occasionally — like if they win a bottle in a raffle (or when we go to special two-fork restaurants where they announce they are getting married).

PS Dale suggested a new BISCUIT LAW that I said I would put forward at an official BISCUIT LAW meeting. I'm not going to tell you what it is yet (because that wouldn't be fair on Layla) but what I will say is . . . it involved a Penguin, a glass of milk and some seriously vigorous sucking.

POTATO—EXPLODER

Someone EXTREMELY interesting-looking was in the yard talking to Janey's mum at home time today. She had mega-short jet-black hair and wore a purple miniskirt with matching super-stylish long, dangly earrings.

Layla turned to Janey and said, 'Oh, look, there's Suzanne!'

I said, 'Who's Suzanne?'

Janey said it was her mum's friend who stays at their house sometimes at weekends.

Then Layla said, 'She's mega cool, Billie. She's a real-life scientist and everything.'

Apparently this Suzanne had taught Janey and Layla how to make potatoes explode and turn milk into a bar of soap the other day when I'd been playing lame baby games with Dale.

'Oh right,' I said. 'That was the day Dale and I invented some amazing new BISCUIT games at my house. It was so funny.'

Although Janey pulled a 'sounds rubbish' face, I've decided I might try to get another invitation to her house - definitely on a weekend this

time. Well, with Mrs McVey being such good art-class friends with Mum S, and me being an experiment expert, maybe I could help this Suzanne learn some new stuff.

OUT OF BOUNDS

The junior girls' toilets at our school are TERRIBLE.
There are only four cubicles and three of them
have serious problems . . . Mr ~~Bald~~ Ball obviously
spends too much time polishing the hall floor (and
his head) to deal with super-essential issues.

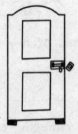

1. BROKEN LOCK
(I NEVER go in there –
way too unprivate.)

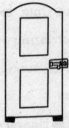

2. LOCK THAT GETS STUCK
(I avoid this one because
Daisy once got locked in it
for a whole PE lesson.)

3. WON'T FLUSH PROPERLY
(So it's often full of
someone else's poo.)

4. USABLE
But often (obviously)
occupied.

Anyway . . . at afternoon break today I was absolutely jig-about desperate for a wee, but the 'safe' toilet was occupied (probably by Daisy Muirhead). I didn't want to wet my pants because, apart from that being mega embarrassing, I'm 100% sure the spare knickers Mrs Robinson keeps in her desk (for Class One accidents, not for herself . . . I don't think) wouldn't have fitted me.

So I had a good think and suddenly had a BRAINWAVE - the out-of-bounds toilet in the dinner centre that only staff and people in wheelchairs are allowed to enter.

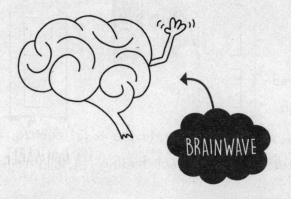

BRAINWAVE

I decided it was enough of an

EMERGENCY
SITUATION

to break the rules.

I dashed over to the dinner centre, crossing my
fingers (and my legs) that the super-secret door
code hadn't changed since last week when I
accidentally peeked at Mrs Sharvane punching it in.

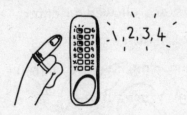

It hadn't.

So I snuck in, went into the toilet cubicle, did my
business and crept out feeling MAJORLY relieved.

Unfortunately, when I exited the dinner centre, trying not to draw attention to myself, Patrick North and Janey McVey were standing right outside the door whispering.

'Orrrr!' said Patrick North. 'We're not supposed to go in the dinner centre at afternoon break. I'm telling on you, Bug.'

'If you tell on *me*, Patrick,' I said, '*I'll* tell Mrs Patterson you keep hurting my feelings by calling me by my initials, so **go away**.'

'What were you doing in there?' asked Janey.

'Having a wee, if you must know!' I said, before walking off to find Layla.

'How did you even get in?' yelled Patrick, but I couldn't quite hear him . . .

I spent the rest of the day hoping neither Patrick nor Janey *would* tell tales because I couldn't risk Mums being summoned for another 'QUIET word'. Apart from anything else, that might have led to Mrs Patterson accidentally on purpose revealing the results of my last three SPELLING tests (3/10, 2/10, 4/10) . . . and that would have led to Mums asking to look in my SPELLINGS jotter . . .
and that would have resulted in the certain death of my STAY-AWAKE DOODLE DIARY.

The more I think about it, the surer I am I did the right thing – there's **no way** Mr ~~Bald~~ Ball would have wanted to use his precious mop on a puddle of my wee.

NOT FOR WEE (OR POO)

Anyway, by home time nothing had been said and all was good, until Mum S said we were 'nipping in' to Janey's straight after school to collect something arty.

As usual, Mum's 'nipping in' turned into about an hour of chatting and unfortunately the short-haired potato-exploder wasn't there, so I ended up having to play with Janey in her bedroom.

'Were you honestly having a wee earlier?' asked Janey.

'Yes,' I said. 'Why? What else would I have been doing?'

Without replying, she gawped at me for a while and then did the splits. To relieve my boredom, I suggested we make paper aeroplanes out of the pages of a dreary magazine about fancy hairstyles I found under Janey's bed.

The magazine reminded me of the odd remark Mum whispered the other day – about Mrs McVey's hair getting up to mischief. So I asked Janey whether her mum's hair was real or some kind of magical wig. She said it was real.

After that, Janey showed me a photo of her dad who looked handsome and moustachey. She said

his name is Pea-Air (quite unusual but I didn't say so). Apparently Pea-Air is soon going to be driving 356 miles up to our village to collect Janey and take her back to her old house for a sleepover.

I said I bet she was pleased about that because it's been ages since she's seen him. She agreed and told me how video-chatting is not the same as giving someone a hug in real life.

I had a good root around in Janey's pen pot when she went to get us a BISCUIT (thankfully not a Nice one) but saw no sign of the one she (possibly) STOLE from me the day I taught her all about ADOPTION.

On our way home Mum said she was glad me and Janey were friends because Mrs McVey had been worrying her daughter might struggle to fit in at a new school.

I decided not to mention how Janey often annoys ~~me~~ everyone, or about her being a possible purse THIEF. 'Janey's OK in small doses,' I said.

PS I have absolutely no idea why the dinner-centre toilet is out-of-bounds. Apart from a funny sign (which made me wonder about becoming a toilet-sign poet when I'm older), there was nothing remotely special about it.

CLOG PIE

Mrs Trapp came into assembly today. She looked even crosser than usual. I wondered if someone had told her the truth about her cat-sick pie, but it wasn't that.

Mr Epping gave up eight whole minutes of his droning time for Mrs Trapp and you'll never guess what . . .

The THIEF has struck AGAIN!

Mrs Trapp said in the last couple of weeks four tins of beans, a dozen eggs, three packets of powdered custard, seven carrots and a bag of brown flour have all 'gone missing' from **HER** cupboard. She put her hands in the air to make speech marks when she

'GONE MISSING'.

said 'gone missing' so we all knew she meant
'BEEN STOLEN'.

The strangest thing of all was when she said a
pair of white plastic clogs had also disappeared.
It's a strange combination of items to steal – I
wonder what the THIEF was planning to make?

Mr Epping was quietly cross this time. He even
said, if anyone had been asked by a grown-up to
take food home because they are struggling to
afford groceries of their own, they shouldn't be
afraid to go to him for a little talk. He didn't
mention the clogs.

I've just had a thought. I had
beans and egg when I went to
Janey's house for tea . . .

 . . . and I've still not ~~looked
for~~ located my special pen . . .

Thankfully, at home time Mrs Patterson instructed
everyone to ensure our money for the hedgehogs
(due tomorrow) is extra-carefully sealed in an
envelope. This is always the case if we bring
money into school, but I'm glad she made
a point of reiterating it as the THIEF (who I
guess isn't Mrs Trapp) is obviously on a mission.

SUSPECT LIST:
JANEY MCVEY
LIAM TABERNACLE
MR ~~BALD~~ BALL
DAISY
RANDOMER
~~MRS TRAPP~~
CALEB

THIEF TO-DO LIST:
OLD LADY PURSE ✓
CLOGS ✓
GROCERIES ✓
HEDGEHOG PROPERTY

FALSE ~~TEETH~~ RUMOUR

Just because they caught me coming out of the dinner centre at afternoon break the other day, Patrick and Janey have been spreading rumours that I am the purse and food and clog THIEF.

Before assembly, when I heard them whispering about it, I told them **AGAIN** I'd just been having a wee.

'Janey thinks we should tell Mr Epping,' said Patrick.

Janey nodded, smiling creepily.

I suspected she was probably grinning because revealing my out-of-bounds-ness to our head teacher might completely put him off the scent

that she is, in fact, the ACTUAL THIEF. I ran
this theory by Dale during our morning SPELLING
challenge.

SPELLING CHALLENGE
How many words can you make
from the letters in 'hedgehog'?

SAVE ME!

Dale agreed. So, at morning break, after Mrs
That's-Not-What-You-Were-Asked-To-Do
Patterson had eventually let me out, I went to
find Layla to see what she thought.

Alarmingly, Janey had taken Layla behind the big
tree and was practically FORCING her to do the

splits. I immediately marched over to save my #BFF from this distressing situation and that's when I realized I had three MAJOR problems . . .

1. Layla looked like she was enjoying herself.
2. The two of them were sharing their snacks!
3. Layla's snack was a pot of strawberries.

I couldn't believe my eyes. I stood rooted to the spot with my sad stick of withered celery until the end of break, panicking that as well as being a purse THIEF Janey might be a complete #BFF STEALER too.

After break, the rumour was getting completely out of hand. I was desperate to get Layla on her own to ask for her advice, so I was pleased when Mrs Patterson announced we were going to the hall to practise our 'Street Dance for the Hedgehogs' routines.

You'll never guess what happened, though. When Mrs Patterson instructed us to get into pairs, Janey GRABBED Layla's arm and pulled her to one side before Layla (or I) had any say in the matter.

I couldn't believe it. Me and Layla are ALWAYS partners for anything remotely PE-y. Well, we were before Janey McVey was invented.

I got lumbered with Patrick North, who (as well as BUG-ing me) has zero dance skills and looked like he was trying to have a poo every time we tried a new move.

As if that wasn't bad enough, at afternoon break
Janey dragged Layla off to
the girls' toilets.
When I followed
them, asking
Layla if I could
talk to her in
private, Janey butted
in, saying, 'Why don't
you go to the *dinner-centre* toilet if
you need a wee, Billie?'

Layla looked a bit awkward but she didn't say
anything.

Although I hadn't had a chance to tell Layla my
side of the story, I couldn't believe she'd think
I'm a thief. We've been #BFFs for six years
after all. There's no one who knows me better.
So I ignored Janey and said, 'Shall we go and
practise our routine for BRIDESMAID DAY, Layla?'

'Stop calling it that, Billie,' said Janey. 'It's BUG-ing us, isn't it, Layla? It's your mums' wedding, not your BRIDESMAID DAY.'

'I'm not the THIEF, Layla,' I stated, ignoring Janey and trying to remain calm despite my stinging eyes.

'That's what the thief would say,' replied Janey.

Layla didn't say a word.

TERRIBLE CHOICES

Mums posted the invitations for BRIDESMAID DAY
tonight. I put a new and much better quality
BEST FRIEND badge in the one
addressed to the Dixon family.
I laminated it this time and
put it on a ribbon.

Unfortunately, Mums put a note in
all the envelopes that said, 'No presents –
just your presence,' which basically means they
want people to turn up without a gift!

I tried to get them to change their minds
because I thought asking for specific presents
like a new laptop, some chocolates and loads of
BISCUITS might be a good idea. They said
celebrating their love with friends and family
was more important than getting new stuff. I
would *never* put this on a party invitation.

I couldn't get them to reconsider their cake
choice either. Not
even when I showed
them my AWESOME
IDEAS sheet.

Personally I think a
three-tiered 'cake'
made completely of FRUIT is a HUGE mistake.

Also, I've been banned from choosing black for
my BRIDESMAID dress. Mums said I should think
about a brighter colour because black is usually
worn for funerals, not weddings. I tried to argue
that they don't usually mind **not** being usual
about things. Irritatingly, as often happens when
Mums can't quickly think of good responses to my
extremely valid points, they changed the subject
completely by asking me how my SPELLINGS jotter
was shaping up, so I dropped the matter sharpish.
But in case I'm pushed for any HARD EVIDENCE...

SPELLING WORKSHEET

Your personal spelling this week is **BECAUSE**

TIP! **B**ig **E**lephants **C**an **A**lways **U**nderstand **S**mall **E**lephants

I'm not 100% convinced of the accuracy of this because what if the big elephant was an African elephant and the little one was Indian, but whatever.

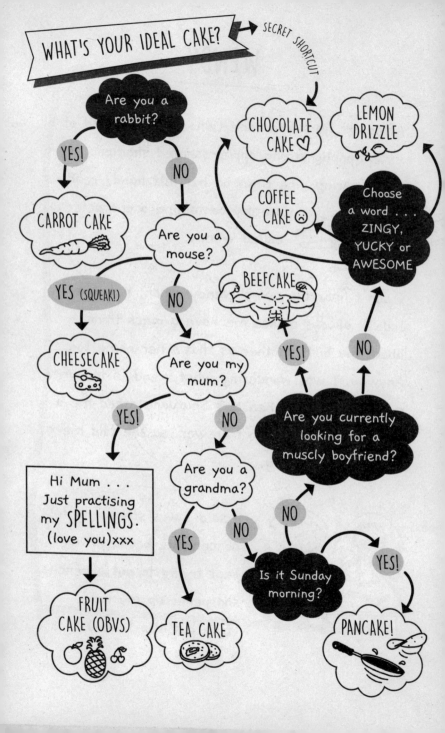

WENDY

After art, Mrs Sharvane (who today smelled of exceptionally strong apple-scented shampoo and was wearing nine rings on her left hand) read us

a story containing a character called Wendy.

I don't hear the name Wendy much, but when I do it always makes me have a quick think about my birth mother as that's her name too. Anyway, I was wondering what Wendy's favourite colour might be when Mrs Sharvane asked me a question that I couldn't answer, so she told me off for not listening.

I said I was struggling to concentrate because Dale kept trying to put a pencil sharpener up my nose (true but also funny).

Dale got annoyed with me for telling tales and I got annoyed with myself because I don't usually break that particular rule.

Before she let me go out to play, Mrs Sharvane asked me quietly if there was anything I'd like to talk about.

I said I'd like to talk about her shampoo. She said she meant anything about myself – anything that was on my mind. 'I've noticed you and Layla are not sitting together today,' she said. 'Is everything OK?'

I decided not to tell Mrs Sharvane about how Janey has been spreading rumours about me that I'm half afraid Layla might be listening to, because that would have involved admitting to peeking at her putting in the dinner-centre secret code the other day and then using it to access the out-of-bounds toilet. Instead I told her I'd been daydreaming about Mums' wedding and wondering what colour BRIDESMAID dress I should choose.

Mrs Sharvane suggested pale pink (nope).

I also took the opportunity to ask Mrs Sharvane why she'd been at Great-Nan's special home the other day. I was surprised to learn that she actually works there as *well* as at our school. WOW. She and her colour-changing eyes (blue today) keep busy! No wonder she has enough money to buy us tiny chocolate rewards.

ENOUGH IS ENOUGH

I'd totally hoped the weekend might have given everyone enough time to forget all about the stupid 'Billie's the thief' rumour.

I should have known better.

As soon as I walked into class, I caught Layla huddled in the reading corner with Janey. I know that doesn't sound ~~catastrofik~~ ~~catastraphic~~ like the worst thing in the world, and I admit my lip-reading skills aren't always 100% accurate,

but unless Janey was telling Layla a story about someone called 'MILLIE' being 'OUT OF MOUNDS' it was pretty obvious they were **STILL** gossiping about me.

I was desperate to get Layla on her own so I
could tell her the whole TRUE story (and possibly
mention how cross I was that she seemed to have
dropped me in favour of a pain-in-the-leg
rumour-spreader she's only known for five
minutes) but at every opportunity other people
kept getting in my way.

For example, at dinner break Farida Banerjee
refused to let me squeeze into line so I could be
nearer to my #BFF. In fact, she was downright
mean about it. 'Oh, **FAB**-ulous!' she shouted.
'Now she's trying to **STEAL** people's places in
the queue!'

As if that wasn't bad enough, when I'd
eventually been served my dollop of
Sausage Surprise, the
only free seat was
opposite Patrick North,
who kept mouthing 'Out of bounds'
every time he caught my eye.

SURPRISE! NO
SAUSAGES!

162

And then at afternoon break, when I ran out into the yard to get to Layla before Janey came out to hog her, Liam Tabernacle jumped out from behind the big tree, scaring me half to death. 'Nice work stealing Mrs Trapp's stuff,' he whispered (possibly trying to cover his tracks?).

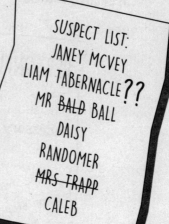

SUSPECT LIST:
JANEY MCVEY
LIAM TABERNACLE??
MR ~~BALD~~ BALL
DAISY
RANDOMER
~~MRS TRAPP~~
CALEB

This simply **CANNOT** continue. The way I see it I have two options to make the whole stupid rumour business disappear once and for all:

A. I could own up to Mrs Patterson about my totally innocent use of the out-of-bounds toilet and mention how the false rumour is upsetting me (as Mums would definitely suggest).

Or

B. I could listen to the very wise advice Dale gave me during this afternoon's personal SPELLINGS time.

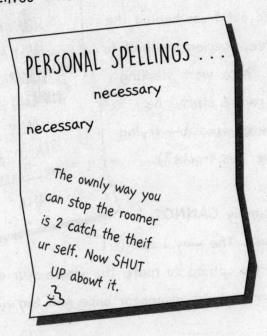

PERSONAL SPELLINGS . . .

necessary

necessary

The ownly way you can stop the roomer is 2 catch the theif ur self. Now SHUT UP abowt it.

I've decided to 'sleep on it', but between you and me B is currently looking very attractive, as A =

UNLIKELY · POSSIBLE · 50:50 · PROBABLE · 100%

QUIET WORD ALERT

SCRUNCHIE BAIT

B won (obvs).

At dinner break
today, having
enlisted Dale to be

ESSENTIAL THIEF-CATCHING KIT

my undercover accomplice, I placed a scrunchie
on the playground bench, then hid behind the

big tree armed with
my binoculars.

Unfortunately, Janey
was too busy teaching
Layla how to do the
splits to take the bait.
She didn't even flinch
when Dale excellently

delivered his line three times from various
playground positions . . .

OH, LOOK, AN EXTRA-FANCY BOBBLE WITH NO OWNER!

Hmph . . .

It wasn't a complete waste of time, however, because, walking back to class, my thief-catching equipment prompted Mr Epping to stop me for a chat.

'Fellow twitcher, are you, Billie?' he said.

Worried the whole silly rumour business had led to me developing a nervous twitch, I stared at my head teacher blankly.

'Birdwatching!' he said, pointing to my binoculars. 'You like it too, do you?'

I didn't tell Mr Epping what I'd actually been using my binoculars for. I didn't even mention how since the introduction of his (stupid) healthy snack rule there's 0% chance of any successful 'twitching' happening in our playground as even the evil pigeons have stopped nosediving for crumbs. Instead I listened to him drone on about the lesser-spotted great tit, then took the opportunity to use this unusually chatty exchange to my advantage.

'Have you had any luck finding HARD EVIDENCE you can use to convict Ja- I mean, the purse, beans and clogs THIEF, sir?' I asked, hoping he might be able to save me a job.

He said he hadn't.

Thankfully, however, he **definitely** hasn't 'let the matter drop' (as Mrs Sharvane had assumed) because he disclosed that he's having some

SECURITY CAMERAS installed in the dinner centre.

'It's a sad business, Billie,' he said, shaking his head before leaving me to walk into class.

I've been having a think since then, and although dinner-centre spy cameras might result in me weeing on the floor come any future toilet EMERGENCIES, I believe they're an excellent idea. Even if they don't catch the real THIEF up to no good, they'll hopefully provide EVIDENCE to Mr Epping about how mega gross most of Mrs Trapp's cooking is.

MEGA GROSS ALERT!

BEEF-BANANA PORRIDGE

BETTER (BUT ALSO WORSE)

The first person I saw when I got to school this morning was Layla. The second was Mr ~~Bald~~ Ball. This order of 'seeing people' turned out to be an excellent start to the day.

Mr ~~Bald~~ Ball, you see, was wearing what appeared to be a dead cat on his head and carrying a large box of cat food (presumably no longer needed by the cat).

Layla and I looked at each other, both pulled very appropriate 'What on earth?' faces, then stifled our giggles when we realized the dead cat was, in fact, a terrible WIG.

'That food'd better be for the hedgehogs and not Mrs Trapp's pies!' I said as Mr (Wigged) Ball entered the dinner centre.

THURSDAY SPECIAL: CAT-**FOOD** PIE!

'We got our invitation,' said Layla once she'd stopped snorting with laughter. 'I can't wait for BRIDESMAID DAY.'

Extra glad to hear this (and even gladder my #BFF seemed to be back to her usual self), I couldn't resist getting a couple of things off my chest before Painy McVey arrived to interrupt ~~our reyoukneeun reeunion~~ us.

'I'm not the THIEF, Layla,' I said.

'I know, dummy!' she replied.

'How do you know?' I asked, wondering if Janey had slipped up during one of their recent secret huddle or splits-doing times, revealing herself to be the ACTUAL CULPRIT.

Layla looked at me, complete puzzlement on her face. 'Because you've been my #BFF for six years! Don't you think I'd have noticed if you'd had a personality transplant?!'

FUN
HONEST
EPIC

HORRIBLE
THIEFY
UNCOOL

'Then why do you keep playing with Janey instead of me all the time?' I asked, hoping she might tell me Janey had paid her to hang out or something. (Layla could do with the money. Her dad stopped her spending money completely when the Dixon family learned they were becoming a family of SEVEN.)

THAT'S IT, WE'VE GOT TO TIGHTEN OUR BELTS!

'I don't!' said Layla. 'Well, not really. I've only spent time with other people when you've been busy with Dale or because you've been kept behind by Mrs Patterson.'

Thinking back over the past few days, I could kind of see Layla's point.

'But Janey keeps spreading it around that I'm the THIEF. Why aren't you sticking up for me?'

'Listen, Billie,' said Layla, pulling me into the line before Mrs Patterson blew her whistle of silence. 'Janey's actually pretty cool. I mean, I know she said a couple of nasty things last week, but she was really upset with herself for that in the reading corner the other day. She's stuck up for you every time anyone's mentioned it since then. She's even been trying to get Patrick and Farida to drop it.'

This was UNEXPECTED news. Although I disagree that Janey McVey is in any way 'cool', I completely understand how mega awkward personal apologies can be. So I went out of my way to be nice to her for the rest of the day.

1. I barely resisted when Layla pulled me over to her at morning break, saying, 'You two should make friends. Come on, let's do a three-way snack share.'

OH, GO ON THEN!

ME

LAYLA

JANEY

2. I allowed Janey to join in with my new game VELCRO—STICK at dinner break.

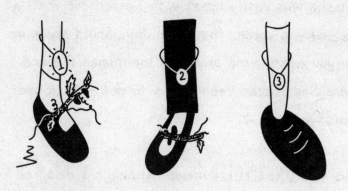

3. I didn't try to stop her copying off me during history.

4. I even considered crossing her off my list of potential THIEF suspects.

HISTORY
The Battle of Hay-stings was a war between some bees in a barn.

I totally wish I hadn't bothered.

At home time I was literally just about to suggest a weekend-long BRIDESMAID DAY dance-routine play date to Layla when Janey McVey proved YET AGAIN that she is still a great big painy-pants (who 100% deserves to remain at the very top of my list of thief suspects).

SUSPECT LIST:
JANEY MCVEY
LIAM TABERNACLE??
MR ~~BALD~~ BALL
DAISY
RANDOMER
~~MRS TRAPP~~
CALEB

'I hope you're allowed to come, Layla!' she shouted across the cloakroom for everyone to hear.

'Come where?' I asked.

'To my dad's this weekend!' exclaimed Janey. 'He said I could bring a friend.'

OMG!

DESIGNER CONSULTATION

Although the rumours about me have tailed off,
I was pleased to take my mind off the whole
'Janey trying to steal Layla' thing by attending
an important consultation with my dress designer
today.

While my stylist measured me from head to toe,
we made small talk about friends. I ended up
telling Grandma all about
Janey, and Grandma
made up a story to try
to make me feel better.

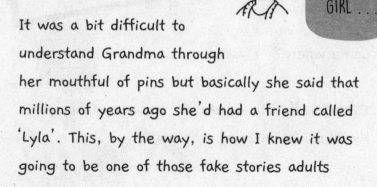

WHEN I
WAS A
GIRL...

It was a bit difficult to
understand Grandma through
her mouthful of pins but basically she said that
millions of years ago she'd had a friend called
'Lyla'. This, by the way, is how I knew it was
going to be one of those fake stories adults

invent to try to make you feel better. If she'd
said 'Gertrude', I might have bought it.

Anyway, Grandma said 'Lyla' was extra popular
and always got invited to parties and sleepovers.
(Further fake-story alert: sleepovers had
definitely not been invented when Grandma was
a girl.)

'Your Layla is exactly like my Lyla,' said
Grandma. 'She's a very kind and easy-to-get-
on-with person who'll always have friends
flocking around her.'

FUTURE
LAYLA

FUTURE
ME?

I reminded Grandma that I'm also 'kind' and 'easy to get on with'. (Hmph.)

She said, 'Exactly! And when you play with other people like Dale or Elliot or Coral, it doesn't mean you're not friends with Layla, does it? Try not to take it personally, Billie. This Janey needs friends too. There's no need to be jealous.'

HA! I'm **in no way** feeling jealous about being left out of a lame sleepover! In fact, I'm 100% GLAD I'm *not* going – Janey would probably try to STEAL my pyjamas or something AND I still have so much to prepare for BRIDESMAID DAY.

Anyway, I told Grandma I'd had enough of talking about it and suggested we get down to more important business.

Our outfit ideas weren't, as Grandma said, 100% on the same page.

What that meant was we had to compromise (and one of us had to persuade the other her ideas were too OLD—FASHIONED).

Once we'd gobbled a few chocolate biscuits, we came up with a design we're both happy with.

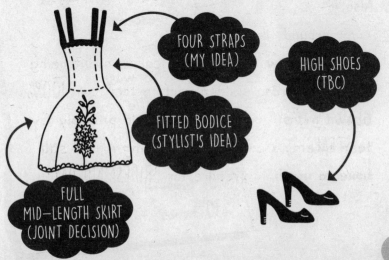

FOUR STRAPS
(MY IDEA)

HIGH SHOES
(TBC)

FITTED BODICE
(STYLIST'S IDEA)

FULL
MID—LENGTH SKIRT
(JOINT DECISION)

Grandpa, who has the main man part in BRIDESMAID DAY, is going to wear a posh suit with accessories to match my dress, including a waistcoat, a bow tie and a cummerbund.

A CUMMERBUND is a big, wide ribbony belt that boys have to wear round the tops of their trousers when they go to weddings. I'm not exactly sure why showing your trouser zip and button is not allowed at weddings, but cummerbunds certainly look snazzy.

Also, 'cummerbund' is one of my new favourite words. 'Spawn', it's been nice knowing you.

TEN FAVE WORDS

1. ~~spawn~~ cummerbund
2. skew-whiff
3. iridescent
4. indigo
5. wishy-washy
6. kerfuffle
7. ~~willy~~ fester
8. ~~aquiver~~ Zimmer
9. ~~topsy-turvy~~ delphinium
10. ~~boobs~~ stereotype

NAKED LADIES

You might not believe me when I tell you this but I've just returned from a weekend away . . . with JANEY MCVEY!

I know!

SHOCKED EYES

It turned out Layla couldn't go with Janey to meet her dad. Poor Layla, her grandpa had already organized to take her and her brothers walking in the Lakes. I hope my #BFF realized what 'walking in the Lakes' involved. Personally I was DEVASTATED when I discovered a couple of years ago that (SPOILER ALERT) zero walking IN water occurs . . .

THIS IS SO COOL.

START

NOT EVEN THE END...

IN REALITY

Anyway . . . when Mum said Mrs McVey had
texted to ask whether I'd like to be Janey's
'+1' guest instead, I
couldn't believe my ears!

'Sounds fun!' said Mum.
'You should go.'

YOU'RE
LYING

'I'll think about it,' I said, doubting a weekend
stuck with the pest who's been trying to STEAL
my #BFF would be anything but terrible.

'Well, I think it'd be good for you and Janey to
sort out your differences before the wedding,'
said Mum. Then, practically forcing me to accept
the invitation, she added, 'But I'm not going to
force the matter. If you don't want to go, you
can tidy your room from top to bottom instead.'

Despite spending a SQUILLION hours getting there
and back, it turned out to be an OK trip.

Janey's old house was totally different from her new cosy flat. It was in the middle of a big city and it smelled of aftershave (the house that is, not the whole city).

Janey's dad, Pea-Air (who wore flip-flops and

shorts when it rained and was obsessed with eating fish), took us to an art gallery and a cafe and we saw a lot of naked women (in the paintings, not in the cafe). He also introduced us to his new bestest friend,

Benjamin, who Janey and I loved because he told good jokes and bought us sweets.

BENJAMIN

WHAT DO YOU CALL A LAMB COVERED IN CHOCOLATE? A CANDY BAA!

Sacrificing my weekend for Janey had other advantages. As well as seeing a slightly less showy-offy side of my frenemy, it gave me the chance to keep my eye on her 24/7, and although she took a very close interest in my new toothbrush I didn't notice her STEAL a thing. Also, we actually had some pretty interesting chats (especially when we were supposed to be going to sleep but the creepy-eyed rocking horse in her old bedroom kept looking at me).

Janey told me that, even though she misses her dad and wishes he hadn't divorced her mum, she's glad she moved as otherwise she wouldn't have met me. Although that was a nice thing for Janey to say, to remind her that Layla is 100% my #BFF (and to help her understand that (possibly fake) flattery wouldn't make me choose her instead) I said she might be able to become a fully fledged member of Snack Share if Layla agrees.

When I asked Janey why her mum and dad had got divorced, she said she thought it was because her dad likes watching the NEWS whereas her mum prefers CHAT SHOWS.

'Also,' she added, 'Dad always works late, so Mum used to get lonely when I was in bed.'

'But isn't your mum still lonely after eight thirty now?' I asked.

Janey said she isn't because Suzanne-the-Scientist is always at their house in the evenings and keeps her mum company.

'Do you think your mum might get a new boyfriend or girlfriend sometime?' I asked.

Janey said, 'Not yet.'

Then she went a bit quiet before telling me she was sorry if she'd upset me when we first met.

I said, 'Which time do you mean?'
(Because, let's face it, there have been MANY occasions . . .)

WHEN YOU SAID, 'WHICH ONE IS YOUR REAL MUM?'
WHEN YOU GOT ME IN TROUBLE AT CIRCLE TIME.
WHEN YOU KEPT TRYING TO STEAL LAYLA.
WHEN YOU SPREAD RUMOURS ABOUT ME WITH PATRICK.

And that's when Janey admitted she'd 'kind of' known two women could get married.

'I just wanted to make people laugh,' she said, 'like you always do. EVERYONE loves you, Billie.'

I didn't get cross with Janey for trying to make people like her by hurting my feelings (despite this being 100% **NOT** my idea of funny). I could tell, you see, that she was trying her best to be truthful and I ALWAYS admire honesty.

Instead I did what Mum advises me to do if I'm not totally sure what to say to someone who has been a bit mean.

I counted to ten in my head and had a little think.

1. DON'T GET CROSS.
2. DON'T GET MAD.
3. HAVE A THINK.
4. . . .

My counting helped me to realize that if *I'd* had to start a new class in a new school where I didn't know anyone, I might have said something stupid to try to get popular.

So I said, 'It's OK, Janey, I understand. It must be hard for you trying to fit in.'

She smiled and we had a little hug but I could tell she was still feeling WISHY–WASHY about the whole divorce thing.

I hope my mums don't decide to get a divorce after they've got married – apart from anything else there's **no way** I could live 356 miles away from either of them. The travel sickness alone would kill me.

SUZANNE—THE—SCIENTIST

Earlier today I was having a serious think about this weekend's homework assignment when Mums announced we were going to Saturday Splash-'n'-Swim.

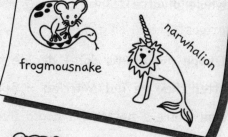

HOMEWORK
Write a speech about yourself and your family. Be ready to deliver it confidently next week.

frogmousnake

narwhalion

And guess what! Janey was there too with her mum . . .

. . . AND Suzanne-the-Scientist!

Layla was right – Suzanne is mega cool. As well as being the only adult to attempt the inflatable obstacle course, she judged me to be the best

ten-year-old diver she'd ever seen **AND** she bought me a grey poo-maker!

100% TRUE FACT

After eating this, your next poo will be grey – try it and see.

blue sherbet waffle cone filled with bubble-gum ice cream

Also, she has three tattoos! Janey said she and Suzanne sometimes design tattoos together when they are taking a break from science activities.

SO THAT'S HOW YOU TURN TOOTHPASTE INTO SLIPPERS! NOW, LET'S DESIGN SOME TATTOOS!

Like my mums, Nicole McVey has zero tattoos.
Unlike my mums, Nicole refused to get her
(possibly enchanted) hair wet. She even YELLED
at Janey for splashing near her . . . at Saturday
Splash-'n'-Swim!

NO WATER NEAR
THE HAIR!

Afterwards, Mums asked Janey, Nicole and
Suzanne if they'd like to come to ours for
lunch and they said yes. We had PANETTONE,
which is a delicious Italian bread pronounced
'pan-a-toe-knee'. 'Words you can easily draw'
might have to
have its own
list at some
point, but for now . . .

Farewell, 'iridescent'.

TEN FAVE WORDS

1. ~~spawn~~ cummerbund
2. skew-whiff
3. ~~iridescent~~ panettone
4. indigo
5. wishy-washy
6. kerfuffle
7. ~~willy~~ fester
8. ~~aquiver~~ Zimmer
9. ~~topsy-turvy~~ delphinium
10. ~~boobs~~ stereotype

After lunch, Janey ushered me away from the adults and said she was worried about her homework.

'What are you worried about?' I asked.

'That I'll sound boring compared to you,' she said.

I thought that was a very honest (and semi-factual) thing to admit, but I kindly reminded her of all the interesting things she could say about herself – like how she used to live 356 miles away and how she has a pretty mum and a shorts-wearing dad. I  also suggested she could describe Suzanne and her cool experiments if she ran out of things to say. Or even Benjamin, her dad's uber-funny friend.

Janey pulled an odd face when I mentioned Suzanne. 'I like Suzanne,' she said, 'but she **always** seems to be at our house these days, hogging my mum's attention.'

Biting my tongue to prevent myself from saying, 'Well, now you know how it feels,' I promised to try to encourage Suzanne to come to our house sometimes instead – I would **never** get fed up with designing tattoos and blowing up potatoes.

MY EPIC TATTOO DESIGN

I also reminded Janey that grown-ups need friends too because washing-up, cooking cauliflower and cleaning cars must get awfully boring after a while.

I think our trip to her dad's was good for ~~us~~ Janey because, in truth, it was a fun afternoon. In fact, although Layla is 100% still my #BFF, Janey McVey is actually kind of OK.

STUPID QUESTION

JANEY MCVEY IS NOT OK AT ALL.

She is, in fact, a great big showy-offy, splits-doing, stupid-question-asking probable THIEF and here is my HARD EVIDENCE to totally prove it.

Firstly she delivered her whole 'speech about her family' from the splits position.

Secondly she went on and on and ON about how her dad has sent her seventy pounds in the post for no reason. (There'll totally be a reason. No parent does something as extravagant as this unless they're after something or feel guilty about something.) Plus, this moneybags tale was extremely insensitive. It came right after Dale's brief speech, which had focused on how he's currently searching for dropped pennies so he can buy his grandad a birthday present from Poundworld.

Thirdly, and this was the most un-OK thing of all, when I had finished my speech she asked me this: 'Do you ever wish you'd not been ADOPTED by your two mums?'

What kind of question *is* that?

I told her 'no' and said '**Next!**' because I was **NOT** in the mood for Janey being like THAT again.

I mean, would Janey ever say she wished she hadn't been raised by Nicole and Pea-Air? I think not. HMPH! Just when I thought she was getting cleverer.

What I sometimes wish is that I'd been **born** by one of my mums so they'd be able to tell me more about what it was like to push me out of their front bottom.

When I got home, I asked Mum if we could look at my special book that contains photos from when I was newly born and pictures of Wendy holding me.

Mum asked if I wanted to talk about anything. So I told her about Janey's STUPID question. Mum gave me a hug and said I should try to be more patient with Janey.

'Try to answer people's questions with the truth, Billie,' she said. 'I'm sure Janey didn't mean to upset you. She just doesn't understand things. You two have more in common than you realize.'

I nodded but, in all honesty, I'm certain Painy (who I definitely only have three things in common with) keeps asking particularly STUPID questions to try to make me feel awkward.

THINGS IN COMMON

1. being in Class Five 2. being ten 3. being female

In my special book, BTW, it also tells me what exact time I was born (4.18 a.m.) and what day of the week it was (a Friday), so I do know all the same facts as the rest of my class, I simply chose to focus my speech on much more interesting topics – like how Mum S can make her thumb bend completely the wrong way.

FREAKY THUMB

RESERVES

Mums have made a reserve list for the wedding. This is in case anyone drops out or can't come. I hope they don't think Great-Nan will be DEAD by BRIDESMAID DAY - she was looking a bit grey last time we went to visit her. She didn't give us any toiletries and forgot to ask me about BRIDESMAID DAY.

On the plus side, if Janey and her mum are too busy doing the splits, or spending wads of cash, or planning their next ROBBERY, or asking short-haired scientists to show them how to make pineapples explode, I might be able to invite Elliot instead.

Elliot is neither a show-off nor a THIEF and today, when he gave me a mega-cool ammonite fossil he'd found on a beach, I told him I loved it so much I'd give him something in return.

I'd been thinking he might like one of my whoopee cushions, but an invitation to BRIDESMAID DAY would be even better.

MEGA—COOL
AMMONITE
FOSSIL

PLAY DAY

Mums were in extra-good BRIDESMAID—DAY-is-
nearly-here/stop-moaning-about-Janey moods
today. So much so that they let me have an
~~impromptchew~~ ~~impromtyou~~ unplanned play day.
Obviously I invited my #BFF.

We spent a bit of time practising our dance
routine, then we talked about how we might
wear our hair for the big day. Layla's got
amazing hair. It's so curly. I LOVE it. If I want
curly hair, Mum has to spend about three hours
pulling it with a curling tong
but I can never be bothered
letting her finish and I
usually end up with a
weird hairdo like this, so
I'll probably wear it down.

Layla's mum, by the way,
is as big as a blue whale.
I think she must be
having triplets.
When she collected
Layla, I told her
this and she said, if
she does, could my
family ADOPT two of them?
I think she was kidding, but
I've had a think and maybe
a baby brother would be nice? I'll ask Mum.

BRIDESMAID WEEKEND!!!!!!!

OMG! What a weekend!

Here are Saturday's highlights:

We travelled to Manor Grove Hotel and Spa in a fancy car decorated with ribbons. Everyone who saw us waved at me. I felt like I was famous.

Walking down the aisle together, Mums looked like princesses in their gorgeous white dresses. I was so proud of them I didn't mention how utterly dazzling I looked once. OK, maybe once . . .

DOESN'T MY DRESS LOOK BEAUTIFUL?

Or twice . . . OK, I mentioned it all day, but let's not dwell on that . . .

Everything was going smoothly until, just as Mums were making their important promises to each other,

Layla's mum gave an almighty and startling wail!

AWWWOOOOOGH!

And guess what?!

Her waters had broken! This, my friend, means tons of gooey liquid gushed out of her front bottom and leaked right through her knickers and on to the floor of the posh hotel because . . .

THE BABY WAS COMING!

There was a great commotion while Mrs Dixon was escorted away from the hotel with all her family and off to the hospital. I tried not to be selfish but I was a bit annoyed Layla had to go. It wasn't like she was having the baby (and TBH I was worried about doing our dance on my own).

Anyway, when the goop had been mopped up, the marriage carried on. Mums had a kiss, some people had a little cry, everyone clapped and, after a BILLION photos had been taken, we all enjoyed our massive posh wedding breakfasts. There was so much food I literally had to leave all my vegetables to save room for my EXTRAORDINARY Eton mess.

VEGETABLES

EPIC ETON MESS

When the night-time disco started, the DJ
announced that Layla's mum had given birth to a
little girl and everyone cheered. I don't know
what they are going to call the obviously
ENORMOUS baby yet, but I expect it'll be Billie
since she decided to
make her untimely
appearance on
BRIDESMAID DAY.

After Mums' 'first
dance', which is
what you call the
first smoochy dance
married people do
after they have
wedding rings on, I knew it was nearly time for
my routine and I suddenly felt nervous about
doing it alone.

But guess who came to my rescue . . .

JANEY MCVEY!

She'd been unusually
friendly since she'd arrived
for the evening do and, when I
shared my predicament, she immediately offered
to take Layla's place.

I was apprehensive about this at first. Well, not
only was there a good chance Janey might try to
STEAL all my attention, but she hadn't attended
any rehearsals. With no other options, I took
Janey to the girls' toilet for a quick practice
and, I must admit, she's a fast learner (and a
pretty good dancer). She didn't even force me
to add the splits.

But then, when we were almost ready to perform, Layla walked back into the hotel with her grandpa! He said Layla had been allowed to return for a couple of hours as she'd been upset about missing my special day. I suspect she was also bored of the new GIANT baby who would have been at least six hours old by then and probably crying and pooing, or maybe sleeping, a lot.

I was a bit torn about who to pick for my dance partner then, but lovely Layla suggested we make it into a three-person dance. I agreed because it made us like the three dancers who shimmy behind my favourite singer, Zakk-O, in his music videos.

ZAKK-O

It was amazing. Everyone applauded after we'd finished (more than they did for Mums' first dance, if I'm honest). After that, Janey, Dale, Layla and I played Copy an Old Person until the oldie Dale was copying started snogging my target . . .

When the party was over, I went for a sleepover at Grandma Jude's while Mums stayed in one of the posh hotel bedrooms. They've decided to delay their proper HONEYMOON for a while, but when they've arranged it all (soon, I hope) we're going to go on a fabulous holiday, probably to the moon (yippee!) . . . with some honey (urgh).

PRESENTS

This afternoon we looked at all the wedding gifts people had brought. I like that a lot of people ignored the silly 'no presents - just your presence' rule as even I got a few things!

My most precious was from Mums. It's a silver necklace with a heart pendant. It's so special that I'm only ever going to wear it for weddings, and maybe funerals.

Great-Nan's still going strong, by the way. You'll never guess what - Mrs Sharvane actually ended up bringing her to the wedding (mainly to help her go to the toilet). I'm glad it's not Mrs

Patterson who works in a special spa home as well as our school - she DEFINITELY wouldn't have let Dale and me play Zimmer-glide on the dance floor.

Even Janey got me a gift! It's a book about drawing, which I first thought was pretty dull (or maybe stolen) but I've just been having a little flick and it actually contains some good ideas — like how to draw a sleeping giant disguised as a countryside. I'm not amazing at it yet.

The gift tag said: 'Happy BRIDESMAID DAY from Janey, Nicole and Suzanne XXX'

Because, get this, Janey's mum brought Suzanne-the-Scientist as her '+1' guest!

And, by the way, I have a sneaky suspicion
Suzanne might wish *she* had a wife because
when Mums were cutting their (terrible) cake
together and blabbering on about love and how
lucky they felt at being able to marry each other
I noticed her secretly squeeze Mrs McVey's hand
under their table. Also, after the speech, she
danced EXTRA CLOSELY with a woman from
Mum K's work who smelled of Christmas trees.

I hope Suzanne finds a girlfriend soon - if that's
what she wants - so Janey will stop moaning
about having to share her mum with her.

Anyway . . . my actual favourite
gift was from Dale and his
grandad. It was a METAL
DETECTOR - a real proper
grown-up one. I didn't care
that it looked second-hand.

TO ~~KEITH~~
BRIDESMAID BILLIE X

I immediately put it to work around the house and found:

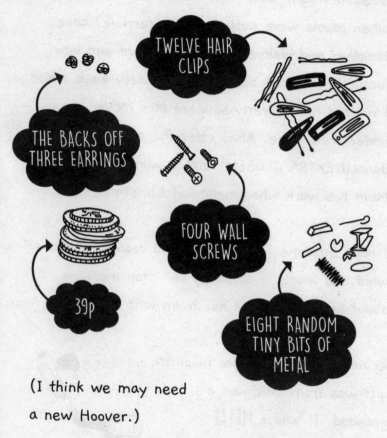

TWELVE HAIR CLIPS

THE BACKS OFF THREE EARRINGS

FOUR WALL SCREWS

39p

EIGHT RANDOM TINY BITS OF METAL

(I think we may need a new Hoover.)

I CANNOT WAIT to try it on the back field and, well, basically become a MILLIONAIRE.

LODGER

Layla's mum brought the new (average-sized) baby to the yard at home time today. She's called Neela (not Billie — hmph) and she's SO cute.

Layla didn't take much interest. To be fair, she had her hands full trying to keep her little brothers from banging on the staffroom window.

After a while of our mums 'oohing' and 'ahhing'
and 'coochie-coochie-cooing' in Neela's scrunchy
little face, Mrs McVey looked at Layla, then
turned to Mrs Dixon and said, 'I expect things
are pretty hectic at home, Carmen. Why doesn't
Layla come to our house for an hour or so?'

'Excellent idea,' agreed Mum, taking her eyes
off the baby to look inside her purse. 'And maybe
we could take the boys for an ice cream
in the park, Billie?'

'Or Billie can come with
us?' suggested Janey.

It was a tricky decision but
eventually I decided that accompanying Layla
to Janey's was worth missing out on ice cream.
After all, although things had been OK between
us since the wedding, I didn't want her to start
trying to STEAL Layla again (or the millions of

extra-fancy beads she had in her hair today).
We watched a couple of episodes of *Saleema
Selective: High-School Detective* on Janey's
flashy iPad and then choreographed a couple of
dance routines in case anyone else's parents
decide to get married soon. Watching Janey
do the splits got a bit boring after a while,
so I asked her if Suzanne would be coming to
her house and might be able to show us some
experiments.

Janey told us Suzanne was at work but would
be 'home' later. That's when we discovered
Suzanne now lives with Janey and her
mum — as a LODGER.

A lodger is usually a person who isn't part of
your family but who pays to live in your house —
normally in your spare room . . .

BUT Janey doesn't have a spare room . . .

When I pointed this out (because I thought maybe Janey was making it all up), she said Suzanne-the-Scientist usually sleeps on their couch.

'We might be moving somewhere bigger soon, though,' she added.

To suss out whether Janey's story was 100% true, I mentioned the house on our street that's

for sale to Mrs McVey. She seemed semi-interested so it might have been true. It might be pretty cool to have one of my classmates living so close.

I wonder if Layla's family are thinking of moving?

OM ACTUAL G

You **WILL NOT GUESS** what's happened . . .

In fact, I'm almost too alarmed to tell you.

So, while I work up to letting you in on the totally disturbing news, I will admit something . . .

I've been wrong about Janey McVey. She's not a THIEF at all. Oops.

You'll NEVER GUESS in a million years who is . . .

I knew something terrible was **afoot** at home time when Mr Epping gave everyone a sealed envelope addressed to 'The parents or guardians of . . .' even though it wasn't Reports Day.

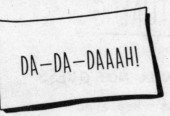

DA–DA–DAAAH!

When Mum read the letter, she gasped and slapped her hand over her mouth. I asked her what it said and . . .

(BRACE YOURSELF!)

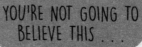

YOU'RE NOT GOING TO BELIEVE THIS . . .

. . . my (ex) favourite-ever teacher, Mrs Sharvane, is the actual purse, beans and clog THIEF!

I know! Also, she's been given **The Sack.** --

The letter didn't actually say that **word for word**, but Mum S said she'd heard something along those lines in the playground (where she occasionally picks up bits of juicy gossip).

OH REALLY?

Apparently Dale's grandad
had heard from
Coral's aunty,
who'd heard from
Patrick's mum, that
Mrs Sharvane had
been asked to leave
our school abruptly
on account of her
STEALING Mrs Robinson's
purse (and probably
Mrs Trapp's clogs and beans
and stuff)

SHE DID WHAT?

WELL, I NEVER!

YOU'LL NEVER GUESS WHAT I'VE HEARD . . .

after Mr Epping (using his recently installed spy cameras) caught her rooting through the kitchens and putting a tin of lightly syruped peaches in her bag for life.

THIEF ALERT

According to the playground rumours, Mrs Sharvane's husband recently lost his job and they've been struggling to 'make ends meet'.

Mum said she felt sorry for Mrs Sharvane and wished she'd known she needed peaches and beans because she would have quietly mentioned the local food bank to her – where you can get

groceries for free if you genuinely need to (not, as I once found out, if you're just passing and fancy a free bag of crisps).

CRISPS
S&V

Mum K said we shouldn't believe everything we hear in the playground and should only listen to the FACTS and, as she pointed out, 'The facts in the letter are only that the mystery surrounding the recent thefts has been resolved and that Mrs Sharvane has left the school.'

I totally understand what Mum K means, as once in the yard Farida Banerjee informed me her cousin's girlfriend had a (FAB-ulous) pet rat that could beatbox while miming the words to 'Humpty Dumpty'.

YO! BOOTS 'N' CATS 'N' BOOTS 'N' CATS 'N . . .

If the rumours turn out to be true, though, I'm going to be so CROSS. Being short of money is no reason to start stealing from your friends. Plus, Mrs Sharvane and her interesting rings, magic eyes and tiny chocolates were something to look forward to on Fridays.

Whatever's really happened, one thing's for sure – the prestigious position of my 'favourite-ever teacher' is up for serious consideration. And, although What's in the Beard? has the potential to be a fun (if occasionally gross) game, I'm fairly certain it won't be filled by the peculiar supply teacher who stood in for Mrs Sharvane this afternoon.

MILK OR YOGHURT?

HALF A PRUNE

SCRAMBLED EGG

FACE TO BOOB

After tea today, when I remembered Mrs
Sharvane also works at Great-Nan's special home
and had even been her BRIDESMAID DAY
'+1' ~~guest~~ toilet helper, I started to worry. What

if she'd also been POCKETING the
old folks' false teeth or, even
worse, PINCHED a couple of my
presents before leaving Manor Grove
Hotel and Spa . . .?

Mums told me not to be so silly but agreed a
visit to Great-Nan's was a good idea,
and guess what!

As we were walking into the special
home, we came face to face with
THE PURSE THIEF herself.
(Well, Mums did. I was
more like face to boob.)

Although she already looked utterly miserable, I decided that I could not let an encounter with the many-ringed plum-scented highly likely THIEF go without telling her how cross I was.

'Mrs Sharvane,' I said. 'I don't think you should have STOLEN Mrs Robinson's purse.'

Mum K SHUSHED me and went red, which I didn't understand as Mum K is the one who always says you should tell people how you feel and not bottle things up inside.

Mum S didn't go red at all. She put her hand on Mrs Sharvane's shoulder and said she hoped things got better soon. That made Mrs Sharvane cry. 'I'm so sorry for letting everyone down,' she whispered before plodding out of the special home towards the bus stop.

I actually felt a bit sorry for Mrs Sharvane after that. I mean, I know STEALING is very wrong, but at least she didn't make things even worse by denying it.

Just goes to show really, doesn't it? You should never judge a book by its cover. Mrs Sharvane didn't look like a THIEF at all. Also, she always smelled so good. Although now I'm wondering if all her fruit-scented shampoos were STOLEN as well. (Or whether she SWIPED actual fruit from Aldi on her way into school to rub into her hair.)

PS Great-Nan was absolutely fine. Nothing was missing from her room (or her mouth). Also, she was in a very generous mood. This evening she gave me two rolls of toilet paper, a huge nappy and a pale blue shower cap.

APOLOGY TIME . . .

I know I didn't outright accuse
Janey McVey of being a THIEF
but in my head I'd been
completely convinced she was
the culprit and it's been
weighing on my mind.

So, to put things right, I asked Mums if I could
invite her over today. (I persuaded them to let
Layla come too because Janey might not be a
purse or clog THIEF but Layla is still my #BFF.)

After the three of us had talked about
Mrs Sharvane's naughtiness (more on this
in a minute), I presented Janey with my
extra-fancy favourite-ever pen by way
of apology. (It had been hiding down
the back of my radiator with four odd
socks and a jellybean all this time.)

'What's this for?' Janey asked.

'I remember you loving it when you came round once,' I said, trying not to look or sound SHEEPISH.

I learned the word 'sheepish' a couple of days ago. It's a word that describes how someone might act if they are ashamed of something, not that they begin to sprout woolly coats or say 'baa' every other word. It's an odd word. But I kind of like it.

TEN FAVE WORDS

1. ~~spawn~~ cummerbund
2. skew-whiff
3. ~~iridescent~~ panettone
4. ~~indigo~~ sheepish
5. wishy-washy
6. kerfuffle
7. ~~willy~~ fester
8. ~~aquiver~~ Zimmer
9. ~~topsy-turvy~~ delphinium
10. ~~boobs~~ stereotype

This is getting far too crossy-outy – I think I need a new list.

Anyway . . . my generosity obviously sorted everything out as I felt better immediately, so I suggested we play Hospitals.

Layla was a lady called Mrs Catagoogoo who was having a baby. Janey was a nurse with big boobs who insisted we call her Pea and I was the bald doctor — Dr Wig.

BALD HEAD =
MUM'S TIGHTS

BOOBS =
ORANGES

Layla shoved a huge teddy up her jumper and MOANED like she was in lots of pain and Janey had to mop her forehead with a wet towel, passing me medical instruments when I needed them.

I said, 'Lie down, please, Mrs Catagoogoo. I think the seven babies are on their way.'

Then Janey yelled, 'These are not babies, Mrs Catagoogoo! They are garden spades!'

We didn't stop laughing for about an hour.

Anyway, back to Mrs Sharvane. Layla's dad is a school governor so, like me, she had some INSIDER INFORMATION to share. According to Layla's dad, Mr Epping didn't SACK Mrs Sharvane at all. In actual fact, she *chose* to leave our school because she was so ashamed of herself. Janey said she thought this was the right decision. Layla said she wasn't sure. I said I wished Mrs Sharvane had been brave enough to stay around and face up to her mistakes. I mean, everyone makes them, and I know this was a

WHOPPER, but I'm pretty sure we'd have all forgiven her eventually. In fact, you know what, after such a fun day with Layla and Janey, I can't help wondering why Mrs Sharvane didn't just SHARE her problems with *her* friends instead of STEALING from them. I bet Mrs Robinson would have lent her some bus fare if only she'd asked. Even grumpy old Mrs Trapp might have donated a couple of tins of beans if she'd known her friend was desperate. I TOTALLY would have shared my snack with Mrs Sharvane

after all the tiny chocolates she's given me in the past. Hey hum. Grown-ups can be so silly sometimes.

PS I'm so pleased Janey's not a thief because she's actually hilarious.

THE NAME'S PEA. NURSE PEA. NEVER SAY THAT BACKWARDS!

EAVESDROPPING

Eavesdropping can be **extremely** interesting. It means listening in to a private conversation that is possibly none of your business and it does not involve dropping an eave (whatever that is) or anything else – unless, like me, you hear something SO interesting you drop the glass you're holding against the wall.

Anyway . . . this evening Mum S took a phone call right when we were sitting down for tea. She'd usually have ignored it or picked it up and said, 'We're about to eat, Mum – can I call you back in half an hour?' or something. But she didn't. She looked at the caller ID, then looked at Mum K and said, 'I'm going to have to take this, Katie, sorry. It's –' she almost said the name of the caller but fake-coughed instead – 'it's, er, it's about that THING we were discussing this morning.'

Well, about five minutes later, she hadn't returned and I was mega wondery about:

1. WHAT that 'thing' was.
2. WHY she'd gone into the utility room to take the call and removed a few coats so she could fully shut the door.
3. WHO was important enough to interrupt Mum eating her favourite tea.

CORNED-BEEF HASH

So I told Mum K I needed the toilet, went into the downstairs

bathroom, picked up the glass from the sink and tiptoed to the utility-room door.

Here's what I heard:

Mum S: Yes, but I really do think it's important to let her snow. (This could have been 'know'.)

Unfortunately, my glass-to-the-wall trick was nowhere near good enough to hear the mystery caller's response, so what followed was basically a long silence.

Mum S: But she's ten years old. She's not a baby.

(During the next bit of silence I obviously wondered if Mum and the mystery caller were talking about me.)

Mum S: I understand that, but as you're asking my opinion I think you should enlighten her. We've always worked on the premise that 'honesty is the best policy' at our house.

(Quite a long silence.)

Mum S: Give her some credit — it might not even be an issue, but if she has any worries, I'm sure Billie will help her.

(As you can imagine, I was EXTREMELY wondery about who I could help . . . and with what exactly.)

(Silence.)

Mum S: Nicole, I disagree. No parent should hide the fact that they're in love from their own daughter. It doesn't matter who they're in love with. (Then I dropped the glass.) Hang on a minute, Nicole . . .

Nicole

(Short silence.)

Mum S: Billie, what are you doing?

BUSTED . . .

Anyway . . . the whole eavesdropping incident led to a long conversation about respecting people's privacy and how listening in to private conversations is wrong. I pointed out I'd heard my name and asked Mum if she'd mind working 'on the premise that honesty is the best policy at our house' by telling me who was on the phone and what the conversation had been all about.

Mum ADMITTED she'd been talking to Janey's mum, but REFUSED to disclose anything further about the conversation. 'It's not my place to share Janey's family's business with you, Billie,' she said. 'Not without their agreement.'

241

She did say, however, she hoped I'd find out for myself soon . . .

I've been having a BIG think since then and have come to the conclusion that . . .

Janey's mum is obviously in love with Suzanne-the-Scientist!

I bet you 50p that's it.

And, OMG, what will Janey say when she finds out? She definitely won't be able to pretend she doesn't know two women can be in love with each other . . . .

THAT'S IMPOSSIBLE.

JANEY = ACTUALLY UNPAINY

When we saw Janey being dropped off by
Suzanne-the-Scientist this morning, Layla and
I realized we needed to have a SERIOUS chat
with her about the eavesdropping phone call.

So at wet break, after we'd finished finalizing
our newest BISCUIT LAW with Dale, we got him
to distract Patrick North and took Janey into a
100% confidential corner to conduct our utterly
necessary 'Can you not see Suzanne is actually
your mum's girlfriend?' discussion.

THE LIMB LEGISLATION (MAINLY FOR GINGERBREAD PEOPLE):

Thou must scoff all face
and button accessories
before beheading, then
devouring limb by limb.

'Janey,' began Layla, 'is everything OK?'

She said everything was fine.

I said, 'Are your mum and Suzanne OK?'

She said, 'They're all right.'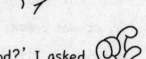

'Only all right or really quite good?' I asked.

'They're fine, Billie!' she exclaimed. 'Shall we do some drawing?'

After bombarding Janey with a dozen or so more questions (that were basically getting us nowhere) and dropping some heavy hints into our pictures (that Janey didn't even notice), I decided it was time to just come out with it. Ten-year-olds need to know what's going on in their lives.

Is your mum in love?

'Janey, I think your mum and Suzanne might be dating,' I blurted out.

'What?' she said.

'We think maybe they're a couple . . . you know, like girlfriends who maybe kind of love each other . . .' added Layla.

'No, I don't think so,' she replied. 'They'd have told me something as important as that.'

So I told her all about Mum's suspicious telephone conversation.

Janey's jaw dropped. Her eyes went as wide as hula hoops. I was worried they were going to pop out. 'OMG!' she gasped eventually. 'You might be right. That'd be so cool. I wonder if they'll ever get married like your mums, Billie . . . I'd love to be a BRIDESMAID.'

'OMG, Janey,' laughed Layla. 'Do you remember not that long ago when you didn't know anything about women loving women and men loving men?'

Janey looked at me guiltily.
Then she went all thoughtful
and said, 'I wonder why they haven't told me.'

I wonder this too. I love that my mums, like me, are always 100% honest. I couldn't stand it if I thought they were keeping secrets from me. 'They're probably waiting for the right time,' I said, trying to make her feel better about being kept out of the loop.

'Yes,' agreed Layla. 'I expect when you're a mum it's a BIG DEAL to tell your daughter you've started dating someone new.'

'Maybe,' said Janey. 'I hope they tell me soon, though, because I'd love to invite Suzanne to Bring Your Parent to School Day – everyone would think she's so cool.'

I told her that being her mum's girlfriend would not make Suzanne her actual parent, but said it sounded like an awesome plan.

We all agreed Janey's mum was probably nervous about starting a new relationship. After all, her last one ended in a divorce and a 356-mile move from a big house to a small flat.

We also agreed parents can sometimes think about things that are NO BIG DEAL far too much so when Janey started to worry about how her dad might feel we decided to be completely unparenty and played Burp the Alphabet to take our minds off the whole thing.

A, B, C . . .

OOPS . . .

I may owe you 50p . . .

Janey McVey's mum and Suzanne-the-Scientist are **not** in love at all. My bad.

Janey (who I've realized is sometimes, in fact, my kind of person) came over to mine this morning to tell me the **facts**!

Apparently on their way home from school yesterday she immediately asked her mum about the whole 'Is Suzanne your girlfriend or what?' thing. And that was when she got to hear the actual truth.

WHAT??!

Wait for it . . .

It was her dad who'd been
keeping something secret
from her.

Wait for it . . .

PEA—AIR

Her dad has . . .

Wait for it . . . .

Her dad has . . .

... A BOYFRIEND

(yes, those two words are
completely stuck together)
and it's none other than
funny old Benjamin – who we
both met when we went on our
mini-holiday to Janey's
old house!

BENJAMIN

Apparently Benjamin
will soon be moving into the old
aftershavey house and the whole misleading
telephone-eavesdropping thing had actually been
Janey's mum asking my mum for advice –
should she tell Janey about it or leave it up to
her dad?

Janey said it was still NO BIG DEAL and she was
just glad it was all out in the open because she
doesn't like secrets.

(I've just remembered . . .
Look back at Page 106 . . .
That must have been
'Pea-Air's antics'!)

Anyway, Janey is so cool – almost as 'It's NO
BIG DEAL' about things as me.

We ended up chatting about life most of the
morning and realized it's pretty cool that I've got
two mums and she's (kind of) got two dads.

She told me her dad had video-called her
yesterday to see how she was feeling about
'things' and she'd told him the only thing she was
upset about was him keeping secrets from her.

I'M SO SORRY, MY ANGEL.
SHALL I SEND YOU
SEVENTY-FIVE POUNDS
TO MAKE UP FOR IT?

She admitted she's a bit nervous about meeting Benjamin again – now she knows he's her dad's boyfriend – but I reminded her about how generous and funny he'd been. 'If you want, I can come with you when you go and see them both,' I said. 'I have a good joke you can try on Benjamin.'

DO YOU LIKE ME, JANEY?

PUT IT THIS WAY, IF YOU WERE A BOGEY, I'D PICK YOU!

#BFF (+1)

After school today Janey and I both went over to Layla's madhouse.

Mrs Dixon is awfully generous. She said she'd give us 50p each if we babysat normal-sized Neela and kept half an eye on the three boys while she went to the toilet and had a bath and brushed her hair and, I think, even had a little nap.

Babysitting was EASY-PEASY.

As soon as we started counting for (fake) hide-and-seek, the boys ran upstairs and we didn't see or hear a peep from them for half an hour. And Neela, well, she seemed happy just listening to us chatting.

Janey said she wished she had a baby brother or sister. Layla said she'd ask her mum if Janey could borrow one of her brothers. (She's thinking about it.) I agreed that a sister might be nice and, get this, Janey said, 'Maybe my mum or dad might ADOPT me one!'

Janey has learned **A LOT** since meeting me.

I guess I might have learned a couple of things from Janey too . . .

Anyway, when the boys eventually came back downstairs we rewarded them for their 'amazing hiding skills' by letting them watch TV so we could concentrate on coming up with a cool name for the babysitting business we're considering setting up. (At 50p per half hour we'd be loaded in no time.)

My best idea was:

BILLIE AND
THE KIDS

Janey's was:

THE
BABY-SPLITTERS

(Nope!)

And Layla suggested
(ahem):

TEAM
BUGJAMLID

Instead of getting mad at Layla's breakage of my number-one rule, I joined in with the rolling about laughing at her HILARIOUS picture.

Janey and Layla tried to persuade me it was so random it was the most memorable, and would, therefore, get us the most bookings when we make our posters. It might be unique but I'm not 100% convinced. I said I'd sleep on it.

Before we went home, we played a quick mind-reading game. Layla was useless but even on the toughest questions Janey was SPECTACULAR.

Maybe Janey McVey can mind-read for REAL in which case she'll now know that I'm starting to think she's my (not including Dale) #BFF +1.

ME

#BFF

#BFF(+1)

BISCUIT JOKES

Just in case I go with Janey to her dad's, I've got all these jokes ready to tell Benjamin . . .

1. What did the biscuit say when it fell off the shelf?

2. What did the biscuit say when it got run over?

3. What's crunchy and says meow?

4. Why did the biscuit go to the dentist?

5. Why did the biscuit cry?

Answers: 1. Oh crumbs! 2. Nothing. Biscuits can't talk. 3. A bis-cat. 4. It had lost its filling. 5. Its mum had been 'a wafer' too long!

HELP!

NO!!!!! This can't be the last page of my STAY-AWAKE DOODLE **DIARY** . . .

I desperately ~~want~~ need to tell you about a majorly important, completely gobsmacking incident that happened today and there's no way I'm going to be able to fit it on a single page. Unless . . .

Forgive me if I don't say 'bye-bye', 'thanks for reading' and 'have a nice life' but I'm going to try my best to be brief.

Dale brought a chocolate BISCUIT into school. Now I know successfully sneaking chocolate into school is pretty big news in itself but, believe me when I tell you, that was only the half of it. The BISCUIT, you see, was - OMG, not only is this situation totally worth more than a paragraph of ridiculously squished-up sentences but I'm almost at the bottom of the page. (Plus, if I write any smaller, even my binoculars won't help.)

There's only one thing for it. I'm going to have to ask Mum for another SPELLINGS jotter. That way I can explain everything properly and our wonderful ~~friendship~~ bookship can continue. OMG, imagine how delighted (and amazed) Mum'll be when I make this request! As long as she doesn't ask Mrs Patterson for HARD EVIDENCE of how this one has helped me, I should be OK.

Catch up soon?

BILLIE ×

DID YOU ENJOY THIS BOOK?

YES

↓

FANTASTIC! Tell at least seventy-six people about it, then look out for the next rib-tickling book in the series, THE ACCIDENTAL DIARY OF B.U.G.: BASICALLY FAMOUS, which will be hitting a bookshelf near you in August 2021.

NO...

↓

OH... Well done for getting to page 262 – I'd have given up way before this. Maybe you'll prefer the next book in the series, THE ACCIDENTAL DIARY OF B.U.G.: BASICALLY FAMOUS (out in August 2021). I warn you, though – it's ten times funnier.

When not reading, writing or doodling,
JEN CARNEY spends her time eating
(often BISCUITS), coaxing her children into the
fresh air (sometimes with BISCUITS) and playing
dares (involving BISCUITS if she's lucky).
Jen is a huge believer in the power of
funny books, especially those celebrating
diversity and reflecting modern families.

THE ACCIDENTAL DIARY OF B.U.G. is her debut
novel. She has been double-dared to write more.

Visit www.jen-carney.com to find out more!

HOW TO MAKE MUM S'S
CHOCOLATE BUMS

EQUIPMENT

An oven; 10 cake cases; muffin tray;
mixing bowl; electric/hand whisk;
spoon; baking paper; oven gloves
(and a grown-up to use them!)

OVEN   X10   OR   BAKING PAPER

INGREDIENTS

200g margarine; 200g caster sugar;
200g self-raising flour; 4 eggs;
chocolate spread

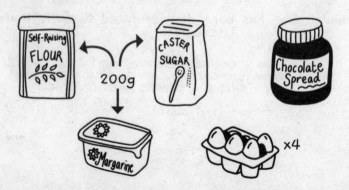

Self-Raising FLOUR   200g   CASTER SUGAR   Chocolate Spread

Margarine   x4

PLEASE SUPERVISE CHILDREN IN THE KITCHEN AT ALL TIMES
AND ALWAYS USE APPROPRIATE KITCHEN SAFETY MEASURES.

METHOD

1. Pre-heat the oven to 180°C.

2. Put 10 cake cases into your muffin tray.

3. Whisk the margarine, sugar, eggs and flour in a bowl.

4. Spoon the mixture into your cake cases.

5. LICK THE SPOON!

6. Make 10 small twists of baking paper and press them into the top of each cake to stop the cakes rising in the middle (to make the the crack).

7. Cook for 25 minutes (ask a grown-up for help to take the bums out).

8. LICK THE BOWL!

9. Once cooled, remove the paper twists and fills the cracks with chocolate spread (not poo!).

10. Enjoy!